Me, My God, My Country

Arthur Desmarais

authorHOUSE®

AuthorHouse™
1663 Liberty Drive, Suite 200
Bloomington, IN 47403
www.authorhouse.com
Phone: 1-800-839-8640

First published by AuthorHouse 12/4/2008

ISBN: 978-1-4389-3804-2 (sc)

Printed in the United States of America
Bloomington, Indiana

This book is printed on acid-free paper.

For Mom and Dad

Chapter One

When I was born in August of 1958, the world was a different place than it is today. Dwight David Eisenhower, one of the heroes of WW II, was president. It was a kinder, gentler world than today. The big war was over and people like my father and uncle's generation had won it. We were at peace. There was still a lot of innocence among the teenagers of the day. Life was relatively simple.

Jerry Lee Lewis was at the top of the charts with *Great Balls of Fire*, as was Perry Como's *Catch a Falling Star*. Bob Cousey and the Boston Celtics were burning up the boards at the Boston Garden, becoming champions. A movie hit, considered racy at the time was Elizabeth Taylor in *Cat on a Hot Tin Roof*. Drugs, sex and rock and roll were not yet fully under way and kids were still innocent. TV shows like *Leave it to Beaver* defined the America of those days.

We were middle class and lived in Manchester, a mid-sized city in New Hampshire. My father was a construction worker and a Korean War veteran. He had come from a large family of nine siblings. His father had been born in 1883 just 23 years after the Civil War ended. He was dead before I was born so I never met him or my Uncle Arthur who I had been named for. He was a Golden Gloves boxer. His name was really Richard Arthur, but he preferred Arthur, so I became Arthur Richard. I thought this was real cool. These parts of my heritage stirred my childhood imagination. How many kids had an uncle who was a Golden Gloves boxer? I guess everybody likes to rise, or think of themselves, as above the mundane like the fact that my grandfather was so close to our history. My father and his brother-in-law, my Uncle Roland, who he was very close to, was a World War II veteran. So our roots were in the old fashioned, patriotic American values. The type of people who would display a flag in the window to show that some member of the family was serving.

This was our mindset and as kids our favorite game was what we called *war*. Basically it was the good guys, the Americans, against the enemy. The best part of it was that we would fight for our country like my dad and my uncles. While it was a popular game of the day it was also a chance to emulate my hero.

We are French Canadian and so there was even more drama for us. On my mother's side my grandfather was English and my grandmother French. This is a group that has its roots in an ancient enmity that goes back to the Normans and the Saxons in old England and Normandy. Why are my grandparents buried in different cemeteries? I don't know the real significance of that but I do wonder about it.

The enmity has carried over to the colonization of Canada by these two groups. The hatred, at times, is so deep that it threatens to tear Canada apart and I don't mean in the spiritual sense. Quebec has gone to complete Franco-ization of its laws and culture and even wants to separate from English Canada. This would be much more possible if not for the impossible political problems that separation would cause.

I often wonder what side of the political spectrum would dictate my own burial ground.

Being French Canadian also meant that it was Catholic school for us. Anyone who went to Catholic school knows the drill. Anything remotely like a break with the discipline received a swift and hard rap on the knuckles with a ruler. Sometimes it was even more harsh. Needless to say discipline was rigid and Catholic doctrine had no room for doubters or anyone who wavered. Several Desmarais cousins had come through school before my brother Richard and I, and I guess their behavior wasn't sterling so the nuns had their eyes on us as potential troublemakers. My father's admonition to me was to, "always tell the truth and if you do I will always back you." If we didn't, and chose to lie, don't expect any mercy. It was a tough but fair policy that I mostly lived up to. Other times I couldn't.

I was a happy go lucky kid but trouble sometimes had a way of seeking me out. I wasn't the class clown. But rather I was vulnerable, I guess.

Like the time in grammar school (Sister School) my parents had to go talk to the nuns at the convent about my behavior. My father asked me what I had done. I honestly told him that I didn't know. Of course to him that sounded like a typical kid's excuse. It turned out to be the Desmarais school time curse as I thought of it. A lot of Desmarais cousins had gone before me and evidently they left an impression. They told my father that I was hanging around with the wrong kind of kids. Evidently my father didn't see this as justified so he grabbed my hand and we were out of there, never to return. This didn't help me with the nuns, and they didn't let up on me. It seemed that in their collective minds I was a trouble maker and it was up to me to prove them wrong. But I was hard pressed to do that.

As I've said most of the nuns were mean and I thought unnecessarily mean. Discipline is a good thing but I think they were fanatical about it. Only one nun fit my image of a nun, and that is a beautiful angel of God in her flowing robes. A woman beyond the constrictors of our lives, one raised above all that. A true bride of Christ, who always wore a glowing smile that lit up her face. And that was Sister Jean. I even went to the school's one hundreth anniversary just to see her again and tell her what her smile meant to me. I was disappointed that she wasn't there and learned that she had left the school to work with underprivileged kids in another state. I thought that she would probably be very good at that. Her beautiful angelic face and eminently kind nature will stay with me always.

Not being a great student to begin with they might have felt like failures at not teaching me better. I don't know. But by Junior High and the public school system, things improved.

Our family, typical in many ways, was not *Leave it to Beaver* typical. Like all families we had our ups and downs. My brother Richard was two years older than me and my polar opposite; we didn't get along like Wally and Beaver. Everything he could do I couldn't. He was good at schoolwork, was artistic and could build things. Of course this left me feeling a bit inferior. There was never any real rivalry between us when we were young because we weren't ever close enough. We didn't play together. Rather I played baseball in Little League, sometimes I was pretty good.

The disparity between us grew as we got older. When Richard was old enough to drive in 1972 my parents got him a car. He used to take me places with him. While that may have at first seemed to me to represent a thaw between us, he would dump me as soon as something more interesting came up. I would be faced with a six or seven mile walk back home. The up side of that was that at least it taught me how to be self-sufficient. He also had a temper. I remember once he beaned me with a rock. I still carry the scar on my forehead to this day.

I was fortunate, however, to spend a lot of my growing up years with my Uncle Roland and Aunt Jean's kids, my cousins, Butch and Jackie. As I said, my father was a strict disciplinarian but not my Uncle

Roland and Aunt Jean. I was golden at their house. I could do no wrong. We were as close as siblings. We even spent every Christmas Eve there. I always felt special in their home more so than in school, where I felt less than complete. I never forgot the family song which was sung more robustly when they all got together and were drinking. It was *You are my Sunshine.* We were closer than most siblings, there was no rivalry between us and they were much older than me. Butch took me hunting and fishing and for rides on his motorcycle. A young boy could never forget the man who did that with him for the first time.

Jackie took us to our first concert *Jesus Christ Superstar* and bought me my first album there. We could also just have fun in the yard or the woods. I was free to be a kid when I was with them.

When my Uncle Roland was killed in an industrial accident I was devastated. It was heartbreaking for the whole family. It was the first time I had ever seen my father cry. Uncle Roland died about the same time as JFK so I could never think of one without the other.

I was about five when I met my first real friend. She was a cutey. We used to go to the schoolyard and tell each other scary stories and then ride home like the wind as if the devil were after us.

Family life could be a fragile thing. I remember once when I was about seven or eight, my father slapped my mother. I know that wasn't a usual thing but they were having a fight and it happened. I know my father was a complex man. There was a possibility that the war had left some emotional scars that didn't show but that affected him deeply. I don't know what the fight was about but I do remember fearing that my family was about to break up and the thought was terrifying. All I was and all I was to become were rooted in my family. The thought of it breaking up was unbearable.

When I was about ten I was into hockey and my idol was Number

Four, Bobby Orr. As you might know, kids judge each other by the quality of their sports equipment. I could never afford a good pair of skates so I gave it up for baseball, but I still have my hockey cards to this day.

My first love became Little League baseball, which I played from 1967 to 1971. I had a great time. The best of it was the feeling of belonging, an important thing for a kid. Fitting in was everything. I didn't get to play much when I was nine, yet the other kids made me feel that I was one of the team. I loved that feeling and I made a lot of friends. I guess one of the earliest insights into my character was that one time I was catching, and a friend from the opposing team was at bat. When he hit a home run, although it was tough not to show it, I was so happy for him. He was a friend, not an opponent and I could feel no other way.

When I hit puberty at about twelve I discovered girls. Still I had no girlfriends for my first two years in the new high school. When they rejected me in a mean way I was crushed but when they accepted me I was in adolescent heaven. I didn't have an official girlfriend until I was fourteen. She was sixteen and the only reason it happened is she chased me. It lasted about three weeks. I guess I wasn't ready for her. Not only was she chronologically older than me, she was ages older than me in maturity. I still think of her today. I had two more girlfriends but I wasn't ready for them either. Whatever girlfriends I had, I was never, ever the one to ask them out. They always did. So much for being shy.

High school is where I made some life long friends, like Pudgy and my wife Doreen, friends forever. I did not realize at the time that forever was not very long. Doreen was the only girl who, in her words, tracked me down, roped me and married me. We started dating when I was a senior and she was a junior. We sometimes rode our horses to school together. How romantic is that? Actually, the first girl I met at the new high school was Bonnie. She showed me around and was very kind. I'll never forget her. I ran into her thirty-two years later when I was cruising the net. The funny thing was, she was the first person to sign my online guest book. We wound up going to the beach on my motorcycle. We had fun, even getting caught in the rain. We never dated, because she was my friends's girlfriend, but are and always will be friends.

When we moved from Manchester, a city, to Northwood, a small town, at first I couldn't adjust to the new high school. Eventually I did. I knew every one of the two hundred kids in the school. I played basketball, partied on weekends and had a great time.

Though I was still shy, and I was the "new kid on the block" in a high school that in its entirety had fewer students than my class at Memorial High School, I seemed to fit in better. Maybe because it didn't really matter what you looked like, how popular you were or how smart, everyone seemed to associate with most everyone else in the school.

I got my license at sixteen. There are few places you can walk to in the country. Of course I didn't get a car like my brother but had to use the family car when it was available, which wasn't very often as both of my parents worked in the city.

Two other big things in my life at this time were my horse and my dogs. I had worked two hundred hours at two dollars an hour to buy my horse. As for the dogs, I joined the New England Sled Dog Club as I wanted to run a dogsled. But the members turned out to be a bit too snobbish for my tastes so I quit.

I had no idea what to do for a vocation after high school and my parents weren't the type to encourage college or anything else. Their main wish for me in high school was to stay out of trouble and graduate.

While I got into trouble with no help from drugs, Richard experimented with drugs and gave himself, and my parents, a lot of heartache. He exhibited all the classic symptoms of a drug user; mood swings, recklessness, lethargy, etc. As I said, it gave my folks as much trauma as it did him. I learned a lot from his experiences and shied away from drugs because of them.

My problems were simpler, like a guy pulling my hair in class and I'd shove him and wind up in the office. I did a little teenage drinking and smoking. But that was all.

In 1974 Richard enlisted in the Marine Corps. The Corps, with its fanatical reputation for discipline, seemed like a good choice and a way for Richard to straighten out and find himself. That may have been the genesis of his rehabilitation because he is all right now.

When he graduated from boot camp at Parris Island, South Carolina, we all drove down there. Of course my parents were proud of him. He looked like a new man with his tan, short hair and Marine dress blues. The graduation parade and the ceremony itself were very inspirational, especially for me.

What has always tweaked at my sensitivities was that when I graduated from Army boot camp my parents did not come to my graduation. Frankly, I didn't expect them to come to Missouri, but I did think they would pick me up in Boston. Instead I had to take a cab to New Hampshire. As I matured and thought about it I saw a couple of possibilities for this happening that should have assuaged my hurt feelings. Is it because the squeaky wheel gets the grease? Is it that the parents pay more attention to the troubled child and not the one who appears less needy? I don't know. But I had to make my peace with myself over it.

I know the old saying that life begins as a *tabula rasa*, a blank slate, and that all that happens to us in life shapes our character and our outlook on life. All that lay ahead of me would prove that to be true.

Chapter Two

If your psyche really is a *tabula rasa*, when does it start printing images and forming opinions about who you are? Is it the first really significant event in your life? Or your earliest memories as a kid?

As a kid I was afraid of a lot of things. For one thing the idea of God scared me. I guess in my childish mind I feared this spooky guy in a white robe with a deep voice who could see and knew about every bad thing I did. It was a scary concept for me. Fortunately my relationship with Him has improved over the years and I think I see Him for who he truly is. But childhood is a scary time. Regarding God and death, I remember that I went to a lot of funerals as my many aunts and uncles began passing away. I was terrified to go up to the coffin, kneel and pray. I had to have my father with me. I would still not look directly at the body but did so only in an oblique way. To this day I hate the smell of flowers. So much so that I can become nauseous. As an adult I have come to realize that life is more about what you feel rather than what you perceive.

It takes a lot of introspection and meditation to get any inkling of who you really are. Are you the person your friends and family see? Are you the image you project? Or are you the person *you* think you are in the deepest parts of yourself. Someone said that the truest assessment of your character is what you do *when nobody is looking*. I can go back to my scary image of God seeing everything bad I did as a kid.

But as scary thoughts go that's a scary thought. Who hasn't done something that you might be ashamed of, but hope it isn't the definition of your character, but rather only a lapse in judgment. Or a bad habit that you are working to break.

Actually this whole idea of meditation and introspection can be somewhat daunting because in the deepest part of your mind you worry about what you will find. Are you going to find parts of your character that you don't particularly like? Are you going to find a person whose ideals you are not proud of? Or are you the type of person who has little conscience and believes that everything you do is right? At least for yourself and therefore right. As for me, I was always concerned about who I really was, not what people thought I was. I needed to find the real me.

In this search I have learned some truisms. Being at peace with oneself ranks way up there as something important to me. I've learned that one cannot expect love unless one loves. One cannot expect understanding unless one can understand. One cannot expect kindness unless one is kind. But the learning process goes on. As I've said we are all a work in progress. This has left me with the feeling that we get what we give and that we set ourselves up in life for what we eventually get.

Of what little I have said of my family it's obvious that we weren't close in that huggy kissy, "I love you," kind of way that some families are. I know that my mother didn't particularly like kids. Probably an odd thing to say about a mother but that's the way I saw her. It was not that she didn't love us, it was just that her interests didn't lay in the maternalistic ways of mothers. I guess her instincts just weren't there for the mother role. Maybe that's why I don't like to be touched. I have no idea if that is why I was shy.

I do know that I was a very guarded kid. I wouldn't let people get to me or rankle me. I wouldn't let them know that they could hurt me. I'd rather withdraw into myself and go play in my room. Or go play with friends and brush it off. I wasn't about to show them that I was upset.

I don't see these as good or bad traits but simply as my traits. Of course others who have to deal or interact with me might wish I were different, but then again, I could wish the same of them.

Back to the things happening in life that eventually came to fill out that blank slate. Now, I realize that I don't know anything about nuclear physics. I also realize that this doesn't mean it does not exist. It just means that I know it exists but I, personally, know nothing about it. It's not something I have experienced, that I could see or feel and so I know nothing about it.

So, I have to conclude that there are other forces in the universe, that while I know nothing about them, they nevertheless exist and are out there.

It's kind of like the Ying Yang of Chinese philosophy. The Ying is the physical, observable world and the Yang is the spiritual, mostly unobservable world, the world beyond what we know of, the world of physics and the atom. The Yang is the world that most interested and intrigued the Chinese. Scientists, of any stripe, won't go near it because it is unobservable and therefore not able to be researched or studied. Except maybe in the experiences of people. Those interested in the nether world have catalogued and described supernatural experiences in an effort to learn more. That, of course, is not scientific and therefore out of the realm of science. It is the world we know the least about, but, as I said, that doesn't mean it doesn't exist.

The Chinese are an ancient people and have evolved a lot of

philosophy over the ages. One of their own was a man named Shao, whose philosophy included pre-destination and prediction. When he saw somebody happy he predicted something good would happen. He had a complicated system to estimate the passage of time and an even more complicated system which made use of hexagrams.

All that is beyond my pay scale as well but that doesn't mean it doesn't exist. I only mention these things in order to make my point that surely certain things do exist that are quite real, even if they don't submit themselves to the tests of our five senses.

This brings me back to an incident that happened when I was in my twenties.

October is a spectacular season in northern New England. This year was no exception.

One fall day in the early eighties I was at my construction site job. It had started to rain as I was working in a thirty inch pipe, drilling holes to blast the rock under the road. When the rain came down harder it stopped work for the day and I headed home. I turned on the radio and the newscaster reported that a little boy was lost in the woods and had been missing for almost twenty four hours. This is critical for a kid lost in the fall woods of New Hampshire. If nothing else, hypothermia could kill him.

When his address was given I was surprised to learn that he was my neighbor. We lived on the same country road.

My girlfriend and future wife, Doreen and I both owned horses. She had a thoroughbred named Fraga. Myself, a big Lone Ranger fan, had a white Arabian who I had been tempted to re-name Silver but instead kept his name, Max. As we saddled up, I told Doreen that if I were lost in the woods, I know where I would be. We headed up the road to the area the search party was in. We had ridden through the woods and back roads often and knew them well. There was a boy scout camp about 2 miles from my house. We rode directly there, crossing the dirt road and through the woods to a clearing that I knew had been used by the boy scouts to build teepees. We rode past all of the other people who had just search that area.

Our eyes were scanning every inch as we passed through the colorful woods. As we entered the small clearing, I spotted a blue color, which was very much out of synch with the Fall foliage pattern. We went to investigate.

We dismounted and walked our horses into the area. The boy was lying on his back in a state of shock. As I comforted him I saw that, although he didn't say a word, he was alright. I put my sweater and raincoat on him. Doreen went for help and soon it was all over. It had taken us under twenty minutes to locate him.

As we rode out, we played the role of modest heroes and told passing people that the boy had been found without mentioning our role in the rescue.

A few days later the Fish and Game Department called on me for some details but again I wanted no publicity. The rescue was reward enough. For me it was the Lone Ranger to the rescue. Of course another element of it was the unknown force or forces that led us directly to the spot that so many others had missed.

The kid had been lost for twenty-hours and we somehow found him in twenty minutes.

That experience has stayed with me over all of these years and encouraged me to keep up my self-research.

I realize too that there is an ongoing debate in society and that is the one that asks the question; are we the products of nature or nurture? In other words, are we what we are naturally, innately, or are we the products of what we were taught, and the way we were brought up? The question then is, could experience change our minds about what we were taught?

I was taught that God is all-loving. His only son came to Earth to save us from sin. When I was in the fourth grade I had to do a report on the Ku Klux Klan. Well, to my fourth grade mind this sounded like a cool organization. The very name Ku Klux Klan intrigued me. They wore white hoods, were loyal to God and rode around on horseback. Again, this sounded pretty cool until I learned what their purpose really was and how they used the name of God to kill and hurt people. To me, God's name was not supposed to be used to instill fear. Nor was it supposed to be used in connection with killing people. After all, wasn't, "Thou shalt not kill," one of God's Ten Commandments?

I could never agree with the KKK because I feel that the most important thing in life is to help people, not to hurt or kill them. I further believe in Jefferson's preamble to the Constitution that we are entitled to "Life, liberty and the pursuit of happiness."

So it seemed to me that I, personally, was about what I had learned and maybe too it was my nature to believe what I was taught. That is, until something more convincing told me that what I thought was true was not. Or vice versa.

At an even later age, I realized that things illegal weren't necessarily bad and things legal weren't necessarily good.

Chapter Three

By now I had decided that every person was a work in progress. It continues to become more clear to me all the time that no matter what age we are there is still a lot to learn and even more to experience.

It seemed that I had developed a sense that told me when certain things were about to happen. This sense, as far as I could tell, was not limited to either negative or positive events. Sometimes it came in the form of a dream and other times it was just a feeling, a sense that something important had, or was about to happen.

One night I dreamed that a Marine had died. I was concerned when I woke up because my wife's brother was a Marine, a Vietnam veteran, and he wasn't in good health. I also had friends who were Marines as well as my brother who was an ex-Marine.

That afternoon I asked my wife how her brother was doing. Looking at me in a kind of wary way, she told me that as far as she knew he was fine. That was when I told her about the dream. About five thirty that evening, the phone rang. When the call showed blocked caller, we hesitated to answer, but somehow felt the need to. It was my best friend's wife. He was a Marine. And he had just passed away. Somehow I could not take these things as coincidence. The premonitions were too strong.

Another example of this sense of portent happened when I was at work and I suddenly felt that something had happened to my father.

So I wasn't completely surprised when a bit later I got a call from my wife telling me, "Dad has had a heart attack."

I immediately started out for the hospital. I was driving on Route 495 in Massachusetts and was just passing under Route 290 when I sensed my father communicating with me. I realized that he was saying goodbye.

I got to the hospital, parked and continued on to my father's room. When I got there, the whole family was gathered around. My mother and I locked eyes and something unsaid passed between us. I said, "I know." He was dead. He had died at the time I had passed under Route 290 and when I had had the feeling.

Now a lot of people will admit that there is something going on here. Some kind of sense of premonition, but they argue that you only get it when something negative happens. That could be that you have a negative personality and you are always waiting for life to drop the hammer on you. That happens if you're the type who always sees only the negative side of things.

But if that is true how does one explain the force or forces that directed me to a lost boy? This was a case of a life being saved, since that kid might not have lasted another night in the woods.

Let me share with you another example of the positive side of this phenomenon. When I was about forty-four I saw a woman's face in a dream. The dream also suggested that I would be marrying this woman. When, a few months later I actually met her I was struck with disbelief. Frankly I had been expecting some kind of hot babe when in fact she was like nobody I had ever met before. She was the epitome of honor and integrity and honest to goodness kindness. As I said, she was unique in my experience. I was awed by her. What makes this experience absolutely genuine is that there was nothing physical between us. In fact, if one knows her one would know that there could not be unless it was meant to be.

She taught me a lot and the feeling I came away with was that I knew her just long enough for her to teach me what I needed to know. Another sense that I came away with is that we would meet again, if not in this world, somewhere else.

I feel that it is rare for a person to experience such a thing and for me it confirms the genuineness of it. And again this was precipitated by a dream.

I always felt I was fated. As a kindergarten student I was walking home from school when out of nowhere a car hit me as I crossed the street. The lady driver was hysterical. She threw a blanket over me and called the police. My only worry was what my father was going to say because I wasn't hurt at all. All I could think of was what I was going to catch coming home in a police car.

While some of these experiences have to do with sensing or dreaming something, other experiences have a kind of message to them. These messages are something that I know intuitively, not with spoken words, but in my gut.

One peaceful afternoon I was canoeing on the still waters of a New England lake. I had stopped paddling for the moment and was just sitting there drifting, enjoying the serenity of the surrounding woods and the calmness of the water. It wasn't unusual that in times like this, I would think of my father. Nothing in particular, just thinking about him.

I always had my camera with me so that I could photograph wildlife or anything unusual. As a matter of fact, wildlife still photography had become a hobby for me which later evolved into a part time avocation. Having a great love for both wildlife and photography I have been able to sell some of my pictures to various media, including newspapers and magazines.

I caught sight of a bald eagle perched in a tree. I had been watching this eagle for a long time. Spotting a bald eagle in the 90's was a fairly rare sighting in New England. This particular eagle was one half of the only nesting pair of bald eagles in the state then. This bird of prey is very dark brown with a white head and tail and a yellow bill. To the North American Indian its tail feathers were considered sacred and were used in their headdresses. The bald eagle is the national emblem of the United States and is considered an endangered species

But on this particular sighting my first impulse was not to reach for my camera, there was something different. He was not flying away. He was in fact, very calm. As I watched this regal creature about forty feet up in a tree, it plucked out a white feather and dropped it down into the water within two feet of me.

I saw it as a gift. From my father.

The Indians always felt that some part of them was in the birds and animals of the forest. That they were, in essence, one with nature. This is one of the reasons why they name themselves after birds and animals.

So was it my father sending me a part of himself? I chose to believe so.

More about things that seem to be fated. After my last uncle died, several cousins and I were in a nostalgic mood and talked about holding a family reunion. As these things often go, however, it was soon forgotten about. Until a friend asked me to go ice skating with her. It was at a place I never go and who was there but one of my cousins, Elaine, who had talked about having a family reunion. That seemed to be the impetus and with my wife's help the reunion was soon underway. It went well and everybody had told their share of family stories and it ended with a firmer bonding by all of us with each other.

Then later that night after everyone had gone home, my wife and I and my brother and his wife were sitting around our kitchen table, having a few drinks and talking about what a great party it had been. Our dog, an old German shepherd, nudged me with his nose to let me know that he had to go out. My wife volunteered. We were all a little buzzed and when we heard my wife start screaming, from where I was sitting it appeared that she was falling down the porch stairs. We ran to the sliding glass doors, I saw her kneeling on the ground holding the dog and screaming, "Bear, bear!"

We had never seen a bear in our area before so I was skeptical, yet I couldn't ignore a screaming woman so I dashed outside. But I saw nothing. My natural inclination was to humor her so I did. Trying to calm her fears I had my brother get her and the dog into the house as I scanned the area. Just as I was about to close the door, the bear was lying at the foot of the stairs, staring up at me. He seemed to summon to me.

It was a kind of mystical moment. Me and the bear looking into each other's souls. Indians believe that animals have souls. Were the bear and I communing about something? What was this message? Did it have something to do with the long awaited family reunion?

The most recent dream happened in March of this year. I had a dream about a girl that I had gone to high school with, Patty. The dream was vivid. When I woke, I started to look for her on the Internet. I spent all day, but finally found her and wrote to her. I waited a week to hear back. When there was no response, I e-mailed her sister (that I had never met). She wrote me back and finally I talked to her. I did not know where she lived but come to find out she lived in the town that I go to every year for a bike rally. We met there it was just like the place in my dream. While I was looking for Patty, I also found Barb and Fran. Fran and I had been together the night we graduated along with her sister Eileen. Fran gave me her number and we talked like school kids laughing and joking. We had not seen or talked to each other for 32 years. We must have talked for 2 hours. It was truly a great moment. The next day Fran called me back, Eileen had died while we were on the phone. I was heart broken and could not believe it. Fran lives a long way from me, but I just wanted to give her a big hug. As soon as I got off the phone with Fran, I called Barb. She told me that she was in Chicago waiting for a plane to NH because her father died. I called Patty next, but couldn't reach her for a couple of days. I was scared something had happened to her after everything that was going on. She finally called me back and told me that she had been at the hospital with her father, he was not doing well. I felt like the grim reaper. We all live in different parts of the country, but it was real nice to make new friends out of old ones. This dream is not over and I do not know where it going. I hope all the death is over. Until I got to spend time with Patty and Barb, I did not know how much I had missed them and their laughter. I was blessed to meet them again and yes, Fran I will be coming to Texas.

One final word on this subject. I've been in three auto accidents, two of them serious, and have never suffered a broken bone or serious injury. Am I just lucky or is God trying to tell me something? Something that otherwise is not obvious to me. Maybe something about how I should look at life?

In the last accident, in a rain storm, my truck hydroplaned on a wet road and rolled over and down a hill. Not wearing a seat belt I landed in a swamp sitting up looking at my truck. A man approached me looking scared to see what shape I was in. When I called to him he looked a bit relieved to see I wasn't a gory pile of flesh. Just muddy, my face bruised.

As he helped me a second person who was a paramedic arrived on the scene. The only reason she was passing by was her vacuum broke and she was going to get parts. She ordered me to be still and stop moving and she held my neck in place and kept talking to me evidently to keep me calm. I asked her if she was trying to kiss me and she laughed. I somehow was enjoying the moment in the rain. Kind people like these two give one hope. They cared enough to stop and try to help. I determined that is something I too would always try to do.

Chapter Four

Right after graduation from high school in 1976 I enlisted in the Army Reserves. My buddy Pudgy wanted me to go into the Marines with him but I declined. Though buddies, we were different in many ways. He was flamboyant and I was conservative, besides, this was something I had to do myself, so we parted ways.

That September I went to Fort Leonard Wood, Missouri, for Basic Infantry Training. Fort Leonard Wood is an old Army post located in the foothills of the Ozarks in central Missouri. For a country boy in good shape, Basic was no real challenge. I completed that and went on to Advanced Individual Training where I was at the top of my class. For the first time in my life, I had achieved a status that I had never done in school. I was the only one in my class to pass the final test. Even though there were only 4 of us, it still gave me the idea that I could actually achieve something and I ended up using that the rest of my life.

I learned that the military can be very revealing about yourself and your character. Somehow, whether it was never issued or I lost it, I didn't have a raincoat. Every time it rained and I fell in without a raincoat the Drill Sergeant would force everyone in the platoon to take off his raincoat and stand in the rain getting drenched. This did not make me very popular.

One day in the mess hall I spotted a raincoat, hat and gloves that evidently had been forgotten. I took the items. Back in the barracks I gave away the hat and gloves and kept the raincoat.

Soon a recruit came to our barracks asking if anyone had found his hat, gloves and raincoat. Our Drill Sergeant assembled us and asked if anyone in the platoon had found this man's items. The recruit was almost in tears. The Drill Sergeant's eyes bored into me like a laser, but I said nothing. After the recruit left, my Drill Sergeant got right in my face and said "You finally smartened up" and then walked away. Sometimes I wonder if the military makes you do things you would normally never consider, simply to make a point about taking care of your gear.

Later this incident was the subject of a lot of soul searching. Had I done the right thing? Was it right for me to allow the whole platoon to suffer for my shortcomings? Or was it wrong to steal that poor recruit's clothes. What had I accomplished? Had I served the greater good of forty guys in the platoon to the detriment of that poor recruit? Or had I stolen and therefore sinned in God's eyes? What was more important, God's disappointment in me or the discomfort of forty fellows?

Now remember, I was the product of the Catholic School system. I was a dyed in the wool Catholic School kid imbued with all that implied. I had received Baptism, First Holy Communion, Confession and Confirmation. God's laws had been drilled into me. Remember also that I had never stolen anything before in my life. I was truly perplexed.

To this day I haven't figure out this moral dilemma. Maybe I never will. Maybe that's what life is all about. Choices. Choices that nobody knows are right or wrong beyond the simple concept of truth.

Anybody who has served in the military knows that adapting to the Army way is difficult. All the things that you consider reasonable in your life are thrown away and things are done the Army way. Some things that rankled a person with a firm civilian grounding was that you always had to hurry, only to wait. "Hurry up and wait," is the Army way. You have to forget any sense of individuality in the service. The individual is nothing more than part of a unit. It's the functioning of group that is important.

Back home I was assigned to my Reserve unit, the 368th Combat Engineer Battalion. During my military carreer I attended service schools such as the Basic and Advanced Non Commissioned Officer School, Nuclear Biological and Chemical Defense course, and instructor training given at the engineer school at Fort Leonard Wood. I served most of my time at the rank of Staff Sergeant.

About this time I came face to face with my moral convictions. One of the reasons I joined the Army Reserve instead of the National Guard was because the killing of the students at Kent State in Ohio by the National Guard (during a 1971 antiwar protest) appalled me. I wanted no part in something like that. I never want to take arms up against my own country.

For a kid whose dream had been to be a Green Beret and a war hero it seemed that I didn't have the blood lust for it. It was at this time that I took on a whole new moral paradigm for myself. It actually went back to my school days when I did the report on the Ku Klux Klan, those supposed "moral" crusaders who wore white robes of virtue and rode around the countryside killing and torturing in the name of God. How many people have been killed in how many wars in the name of God? While I had a Catholic school education I didn't need one to know that God isn't about killing, nor is He about fear. He didn't come to Earth to kill but to save mens' souls.

While any reader of Scripture knows that one of God's Commandments is, "Thou shalt not kill," it never really had been satisfactorily translated for me. Does that mean that you should not kill, ever, even in defense of yourself and your loved ones? Does it mean you should not kill in war in defense of your country? Does it mean that abortion is murder? Does it mean that it is okay for the state to kill a murderer, or is that always wrong, even if the murderer has slaughtered numerous people in the most heinous way?

Even struggling with this ambiguity I understand that in most cases, short of the above, killing is wrong.

My philosophy evolved into the idea of *Be kind to others even if they are not kind to you.* You will be the better person for it. This line of thinking also evolved into the concept that life is not about me but about you. It is better to stop and help someone else.

As I said, my uncles fought in WWII, my father fought in Korea, many cousins fought in Vietnam, my brother enlisted in the Marines and I in the Army. We were, undoubtedly, a patriotic family. I was only a kid during the Vietnam War and maybe my thinking was immature but I saw the war protesters as bad people. I felt like my country deserved better.

From my immature and innocent point of view, fighting for one's country was an honor. Lots of mature people felt the same way.

Of course as an adult I realize that the question wasn't quite as simple as I put it as a kid. One could be sucked into the wrong war at the wrong time.

One of the few times I saw my father shed tears was when his sons went off to serve their country. He knew about war as only an old veteran can. He suffered and lost buddies in the frigid wasteland of North Korea. He knew of the suffering and pain of war. Nobody can tell an old warrior about war. His point of view was that if you really wanted to consider going to war you had to be willing to put your own son or daughter on the beach first. That was a sobering thought and I still think about it when old politicians talk about going to war.

I attribute this more logical reasoning about war to my father. Before his advice I don't think I ever really thought about the implications of war. Yet during his lifetime we agreed on little. Whatever side of an issue I was on, he was on the other. Maybe this is just the way of fathers and sons. Still I was appreciative of him planting the idea of thinking about things, rather than just accepting.

At some point in my youth I became interested in the idea of God and country and the interaction between them. So I went to the library and did some reading. Several figures out of American history impressed me with their dedication to this concept.

There is little doubt that Abraham Lincoln was a great president and an even greater man. I was impressed with his eloquent and profound interpretation of God and country and how the two are bound. Love of God. Love of country. For me Lincoln was as great as the great country he presided over. There was more bloodletting in the Civil War, which Lincoln pursued, than at any other time in American History before or after. Yet the cause, if any cause can ever be, was noble. If the war was not fought this would be a much different country today.

Another figure in the same mode was General Douglas MacArthur. In his farewell speech to the cadets at West Point he said, "I'm just a soldier who tried to do his duty as God gave him the light to see that duty."

No one can doubt his dedication to God and country. In a world of flawed mortals these men stood out above the rest because of their dedication to the principle of God and country.

When I took my oath of allegiance going into the Army in 1976 I meant it then and I mean it now. I just want to know, or rather, be sure who my enemy is. And why I have to fight him. I think in this enlightened age of instant communication no politician can advocate for war without a very strong case backed up by facts. Not conjecture.

I learned more about myself with Army service. There were few to no blacks in our high school in New Hampshire, so I had formed no opinions about race. While in the service I learned to value a person for their good qualities and that alone. Race was never an issue for me, and while that was natural to me, in this day and age I am proud of that.

Earlier I described how one loses their individual identity in the service. Still there are times when a man's decision is his and his alone.

Back in 1987 my unit was deployed to Honduras in Central America. While there was turmoil in the country our mission was to build roads. One day before a couple of us set out in a pick-up truck for another work site our Commanding Officer told us that we could travel nowhere in the country without our weapons and ammunition. While this didn't set well with me, as usual, I obeyed orders.

I was sitting in the back of the pick-up with our radio. While we were driving down the road a guy leaped into the back with me. He was armed with a machete and began waving it and threatening me with it. My M-16 was locked and loaded. I used it to ward him off. It was a frightening and tense situation. I was scared and though I certainly could have, the thought of shooting him never crossed my mind, rather I yelled for the driver to speed up. He did and the insurgent, or whoever he was, fell off the truck, much to my relief.

That experience could have clouded my judgment about the Honduran people but it didn't. I loved the kids. They were cute and very curious and would always crowd around us wherever we met them. I bought them sodas and cookies and always wondered why they scooted off with them. I asked somebody why they did that and learned that they brought the goodies home to their fathers. After that I made them eat and drink with me.

I came to realize that while I knew a lot more about the world out there than these people did, I knew nothing of them.

Looking back on my military experience I had and still have, some reservations about orders and whether it is freedom we defend or something else. As much as not being able to leave camp without weapons and not knowing why. I had 12 guys with me, all asking me why, and I didn't have the answer. And yet their safety was my responsibility. I was 29 and being led blindly, I did not like that at all. The news was blacked out and I wondered who they thought I was going to tell, being in the middle of nowhere. There was a sense of paranoia about standing in the open and watching the kids and adults around you that, just yesterday was fun and games. Now it had become something else. I wondered after that if the only reason the native people liked us was because we had the power. Most people don't want to piss off the guy with the gun. I never had a problem dying for my country. So many had done it before me. I guess I just wanted to make sure it was for something good. I never thought the line "I was just following orders" was really a good excuse, having watched Vietnam on TV growing up and how the soldiers were treated at home. They had fought with honor and our country did not, so I saw myself in the beginning of another Vietnam. I know it sounds stupid, but thank God it did not happen. My whole life I was never really a guy who did things just because someone said so, whether it was my friends or parents, I first had to be convinced, if it did not feel right to me it was not going to happen. In my case it helped and hurt. I have lost friends over it with great sadness Mike, Jim, Tom, these were and are good people and I think about them often. Sometimes I wonder if right is right all the time or is there something else that I am overlooking? Or is right like freedom, honor, truth, respect? All these words seem to have a different meaning to everyone who is right and who is wrong. The only thing I have to go on is what I know inside. I don't know if I am right but I don't think I am wrong.

Freedom as a concept doesn't really exist. One has to give up some freedoms in a society like America because freedom here is about responsibility and respect that we pass to each other. A solider gives up his freedom to fight wars willingly and sometimes not. Freedom is a valuable thing and we as Americans believe it is our right. But it is not. It costs. And we are finding that out with every conflict we get involved in. Freedom seems to be a natural right, at least our forefathers thought so. Freedom gives us the ability to have thoughts, express those thoughts and to do so without fear of retribution as is the case in so many countries around the world.

So for mankind "freedom" is a concept that is in the heart and soul of all humans. We saw that in China with the tanks and protesters. The idea of freedom will not go away, no matter how many tanks and guns are aimed at it. Freedom requires people paying attention, for we see what happens when we don't. In some ways we only have ourselves to blame. For freedom to work it also requires you to allow me to be free and I in turn I allow you to be free without fear.

While by 1990 I had some doubts and reservations about how my country was handling things in the Middle East, I still wanted to go and to serve. It was only when our unit, which rumor had it was to be deployed to Kuwait and, ultimately was not, was when I finally resigned from the Army Reserve.

Chapter Five

Even as I grew to maturity I had always been guided and inspired by our famous forefathers and most of all, the United States Constitution. The things it espoused were so fair and decent that it took on a religious significance for me, a kind of reverent devotion to its principles. And I learned that the more I examined the world around me and wanted to understand it, I found that the deeper I needed to search my soul. And I use that term in its most honest sense.

In my childhood innocence I looked on the Constitution as sparkling white in its purity and further I believed it reflected the values of the American people.

Of course when one does some serious soul searching it becomes clear that Man as a species is most imperfect. As a Catholic I realized this because I was taught that only God himself was perfect. Therefore the Constitution with all its fairness and purity was so idealistic that it was almost impossible for humans to adhere to. At least strictly. Sure, many could echo its principles and values but few could actually live it. In some ways it is like the Catholic Church itself. Recent events have proved that some priests acting as the embodiment of Christ's church were no doubt falling short. That is not to say that a small percentage of wrongdoers reflect the whole body of men who represent God's church in the Catholic faith here on earth. That is an unfair condemnation of a two thousand year old Church with a wonderful record of helping humanity in practical and financial ways around the world. Few dispense as many goods and services and inspiration as Catholic Charities. In this way they are truly doing God's work. Of course, much the same can be said for churches of other faiths, but it is the few perverted Catholic priests who tarnish the entire church by their actions. And it is this same church which has received most of the condemnation. The Church of Peter's ideals are high and many falter as they try to live up to them. Funny, for a kid who always wanted to be a Green Beret, I never thought I'd adopt the role of Protector of the Faith.

This seems to be a good place to discuss my feelings about the separation of Church and State. I've already said that I have a reverence for our nation's forefathers and the brilliant piece of work, the U.S. Constitution that they produced.

Now the part about separation of Church and State is very simple but it has been perverted, twisted, misconstrued and out and out lied about since its inception back in the eighteenth century.

First, take a look at the history that had prompted the forefathers to include such a principle as Separation of Church and State. The people's forbearers were mainly English. In the sixteenth century all of England was Catholic. The English king, Henry the Eighth, unable to produce a male heir to the throne of England, asked the then sitting Pope for a divorce so he could remarry and produce a male heir. The Pope, sticking to the dogma of the Church refused. In retaliation Henry broke with the Church and formed his own church, the Church of England, branch of the Protestant Church. The followers were called Anglicans. All this happened during the Reformation in Europe where Martin Luther founded Protestantism.

As a result of this move, England acquired all of the Papal lands (land was the main form of wealth back then) in the British Isles, making him immediately one of the wealthiest monarchs in Europe.

Those Catholics who continued to practice their faith in the British Isles were persecuted. It was sometimes physical but mostly more subtle. For example, Catholics couldn't get high ranking government jobs or even deliver mail. It caused many, like our own Pilgrims, to immigrate to North America and elsewhere.

Our own forefathers, knowing this, simply meant by Separation of Church and State was that "Congress shall pass no laws respecting an establishment of religion or to prohibit the free exercise thereof."

While this was written in the language and parlance of the times, it did not mean that there could be no utterance of any particular religion publicly. What it simply meant was that the *State could not enforce the practice of any particular religion for the American people.* This was done to ensure that our system would not be the same as the former motherland which persecuted people who were not Anglicans. Further, the American system guaranteed that you could practice any religion you wanted to without interference from the state.

So, as mentioned before, "Democracy is the worst of all systems, but it's the best in the world." What was meant by this is that democracy can be so easily perverted because every person is able to express his feelings and speak his mind. In the heat of elections and the give and take of public opinion, the Separation of Church and State today has come to mean something entirely different from the intentions of the forefathers.

Today they remove the Nativity scene from a public square where it has been displayed for hundreds of years. Why? Because they say it is as though everyone (Jews, Muslims, etc) is worshipping the *Catholic* religion. The Christian cross is being challenged everywhere it can be seen publicly. There is so much religion in the language of our laws that it is impossible to remove it everywhere. Take American paper money, (and coins too) which has emblazoned across it "In God We Trust." Which God is this? The God of Abraham? Peter? Mohammed? See the perversion?

In Alabama, the plaque of The Ten Commandments outside a courthouse was construed to violate Church and State and was removed. Similar attempts are going on all the time.

An atheist in California sued the US Government for requiring his daughter to pledge allegiance to the flag. Now that is a bit of a departure from Church and State but you can see where it is going. Again it's people trying to change things. Sometimes simply because they want to. So the blessings of Democracy itself are perverted by people's selfish wishes.

This is not what the forefathers intended, but people today interpret things in their own best interest.

Of course one of the problems is that the world of the 18th Century is far different from the 21st Century and things that might have seemed so right back then no longer keep up with the necessities of modern times. In this sense, change is legitimate, but legally only after a lengthy public debate can our Constitution be amended. And many purist readers of the Constitution will fight even that. But there have been Amendments and if the people wish for religion to be separated in this way it should take a Constitutional Amendment to do it. Right after 9-11 a friend of mine, who was pastor of a church, told me that the parishioners wanted to bring flags and sing patriotic songs. She said no. She told them God is not about country but about people. Just a thought.

And so as it goes for the Church, it goes for the Constitution. Some of my study revealed that some of the most corrupt, repressive regimes on earth (the old Soviet Union and China for example) had constitutions that closely resembled the U.S. Constitution in almost every detail. But what good is it (as with these examples) if a country doesn't at least attempt to live up to these ideals. And so it goes for the Church.

As for who is fighting for God and who isn't, I think every man has his own God. But the scary thing is that when one claims he is fighting for God, who is right? There is a saying in the military. "Kill them all and let God sort them out."

And another anti war sentiment made by a great warrior, Union General William Tecumseh Sherman. "Make war so much hell they won't want to fight again for another one hundred years."

Maturity brought more revelations. I found that many social policies of the US Government, while sounding high minded and supposedly written for the benefit of everyone, are in real life not available to everyone. So while social justice is a high ideal, we are far from it in many places, although in recent years we have made great strides toward it.

It would be hard for anybody to argue that the rich and mighty do not live by the same set of rules that the middle class or the poor live by. The truth is that not every smart, deserving kid can get into an Ivy League school. Family connections and political ties have a lot to do with it. Yet that's not what our Constitution says.

Job discrimination is supposed to be illegal. But we all know it is practiced. Those with connections get the jobs that those without cannot get. Even on a subliminal level studies have shown that tall, attractive people are more likely to be hired for most jobs than short, unattractive people.

Now, let's consider an even more pressing concern. The United States going to war. Nobody doubted the righteousness and need for us to go to war after the Japanese attacked Pearl Harbor. We were truly faced by an axis of evil. But America was a different country back them. People, in general, were less prone to doubt the wisdom of their government's policies. And in the case of WWII it is hard to argue that we would indeed be living in a different world had we not won against the Axis of Evil.

George Bush tried to apply the same reasoning in going to war against a new Axis of Evil in the twenty first century. But things are different today. In an age of instant communication people are better informed and not so willing to take the government at its word. This is no doubt a good development. For it will keep us out of needless wars. Except when the government is truthful with us and makes a cogent and compelling case that it is the right thing to do.

That brings me to the subject of Vietnam. I had seven cousins and a lot of friends who fought and some of them died in Vietnam. On a recent trip to Washington, DC and the Vietnam Memorial Wall I saw grown men run their fingers over various names with tears in their eyes. It was a savage war that cost us more than 50,000 dead, and many more countless thousands who are suffering from various stages of post-traumatic stress, including members of the families of soldiers like their spouses and children. I was to learn later during my own deployment to Honduras that what men fought for weren't the time-honored patriotic principles that I so cherished as a child, but for a different reason. Men fought for one another. You were in it with your buddies and you would do anything for them as they would for you. In that sense all my childhood ideals that soldiers fought for God and country proved untrue. It was an idealistic idea that went the way of many other such ideals. The reasoning was that we fought the war in Korea for the same reason. To stop the rise of Communism.

My father fought in Korea and he was one of the lucky ones to return alive. We lost about 38,000 men. For what? The status quo!

Korea is the same peninsula today with a Communist north and a Democratic south. Can we call it a success? Well, if nothing else we could call it a draw. This, at least, was better than Vietnam. After all, although the U. S military won every battle and major engagement in Vietnam, for whatever reason we lost the war. Many will blame the American press and the anti war movement back home. And a lot of that is true, but still the government should have known better than to engage in an Asian war with a fanatical enemy without any clear strategy for ever winning the war.

Now I'm not saying that these wars should not have been fought, but what I am saying is that there was a certain amount of dishonesty by the U.S. government to get us into them. In Vietnam, President Johnson was able to escalate the war by claiming (much proof exists to refute this) that North Vietnamese PT boats attacked our ships in the Gulf of Tonkin. This action led us to convene Congress and adopt the Gulf of Tonkin Resolution, which was no more than a call to arms under false pretenses.

Today, what is happening in Iraq reflects many of the same lessons of history. Saddam Hussein was no doubt one of the worst, most evil dictators around. But the premise for ousting him was not entirely truthful. I say not entirely, because there were some other compelling reasons. But the point is the American people should have known the full truth before the country was committed to the war.

After 9-11 we all wanted to kick someone's ass and quite frankly we didn't care whose it was. I can't blame President Bush for feeling the same way. Most of the people around me were saying the same thing. Kick their ass. I for one thought that guy in Iraq was nothing to us. And I saw this as another Vietnam. Besides, we can't save them unless they want to be saved. Revolutions have to begin with the people of the country. We can hardly inspire revolution or inspire them with our own ideals, although many think we can. The Iraqis and only the Iraqis have the right and desire to seek self determination. Of course from the United States point of view it would be advantageous for us to have a working democracy in the heart of the Middle East. But even with the overthrow of the Fascist government of the dictator, Saddam Hussein, there is still no peace here at home in America.

My study of history tells me one thing. It's all about power. Our own Civil War was more about power than it was about States Right's, Slavery, or was it just about not having the Northern majority telling the South what to do. What was States Rights all about? State and local power. They didn't like giving up any of it to the Federal government.

This too is what's going on in Iraq. How they differ for us is that we had a common bond. They are separated by religion, Shiite against Sunni, against Kurd. With them it's which group lives in the area where there is the most oil wealth.

So Abraham was right about us. "Our forefathers did bring forth on this continent a new nation conceived in liberty and dedicated to the proposition that all men are created equal." And that this nation will continue to be tested and fail at times but we will learn from our mistakes and the people will watch their government to make sure that the power we gave them will be used for good, not only here but all over the world.

The bottom line is that it is much easier to get into these quagmires than it is to get out. We are learning that the hard way in these post WWII conflicts. The government needs to act not upon fear but upon logical information, for when we act upon fear we only create fear.

Regarding social and economic policy, how is it that the country that could muster the resources to go to the moon in 1969 still cannot figure out a way to make us independent from needing foreign oil? Most of the conflicts in the Middle East, while fueled by Islamic

Fundamentalism, still evolve around oil and its use as a medium of power.

I do agree that the primary job of any government is the responsibility to keep its people safe. What good are benefits if one isn't alive to enjoy them? In this I am in complete agreement with those who maintain this policy. However, I don't necessarily believe that in order to be safe we should employ a first strike policy. Who was it? Teddy Roosevelt, our twenty sixth President who said, "Walk softly and carry a big stick." Now that's a policy I can sign on to.

My own military deployment to Honduras taught me a lot. It takes foreign experience to realize how rich we are and how poor many countries, especially Third World countries, are. In Honduras I remember a kid begging to shine my boots for 25 centavos.

I let him do it because I am a lazy American who could get his boots shined for about 15 cents! But then I began to feel uncomfortable as if I was using some kind of slave labor. When I tried to stop him he began shouting, "No good job? No good job?" He thought I was complaining that he wasn't doing a good job. Now I'm not a big guy but he was so small and scrawny that I could pick him up with one hand, which I did trying to make him understand but the language barrier made it difficult.

I promised him twenty-five centavos *not to shine my boots*. That was hard for him to understand but he finally got the knack of it. So, every day he came by and I gave him the twenty-five centavos. This experience made me realize how rich we are as a people and a country. You need a point of comparison and that little kid in the poor Central American country of Honduras was the comparison for me. I was very much aware of the world around me but not the world around the boy.

It was also at this time I realized the generosity of the American soldier and by way of heritage the American people themselves. We were warned by our Commanding Officer under threat of punishment (Article 15 of the Military Code) not to give food to the natives. Still, every day as we left our camp we threw food to the people along the road.

The warnings continued but it did not stop the soldiers from giving away the food. Finally the CO gave up. It wasn't worth it to try to enforce such a regulation.

Another example of this is this scenario. One night one of our tractor trailer trucks carrying pipe went missing on its return from Palmerola Air Force Base. It was obviously down the jungle road, broken down or out of gas. The helicopter pilots had orders not to fly at night. So what did they do? They took off anyway, found that the truck had gone over an embankment and they rescued the driver who was flown to Panama with serious injuries. If the rules and regulations were enforced this rescue flight by the helicopter pilots would have been considered a court martial offense and a blot on the pilot's record. Yet he decided to do what he thought was right. Now I realize the value of rules and regulations, but I also admire the spirit of aiding those in need.

This experience helped re-inforce my notion that all rules aren't right just because they are rules. The spirit of people is more important. This is why I love Americans. Every American soldier would be willing to save another, even if it meant his own possible death.

After all, why are rules written in the first place? They are written to fulfill a need. But times change and the needs of yesterday may not necessarily be the needs of tomorrow.

Rules and regulations, while they are written to be respected, should never be considered sacrosanct. That is to believe they are flawless. They are only the product of flawed Mankind and so are susceptible to

Me, My God, My Country

being wrong, or need to be changed for newer times.

My point with all of this is not to give the impression that I have the answers for all the great challenges facing my country. But rather it is to give the gut feeling of one citizen soldier. It's hard to argue against what all of us know by sheer instinct: that sometimes gut instincts are the best.

Chapter Six

It's a revealing thing, this introspection. If you search deep and stick with it and challenge your memory you tend to learn much about yourself and how you have evolved. Some of the things you had long forgotten.

I started out in my youth as a gung ho, John Wayne American. There's nothing wrong with that I suppose. I liked Superman and the all American way too. Except that with maturity comes the realization that these icons of the American right are too simplistic for our complicated world. Of course maturity comes at different times for different people.

First and foremost I have come to realize that I always wanted people to like me. I guess that's a natural thing. Yet I have also come to realize that in order for people to like you, one has to like himself. When I was a kid in Catholic school, I thought the nuns were mean to me because they didn't like me. I noticed that they weren't mean to everybody and so I surmised they must not like me. I have come to realize that I didn't fit their mold. I wasn't with their program. I wasn't a success for them since I was an enemy of strict rules and regulation as a kid. I was just the little kid who sat next to you in class. I may have thrown a couple of paper airplanes around class or played football on the desk, especially after they got rid of the old desks with the ink wells.

I was the one who never raised a hand to answer a question or ask you out. I would share my candy on Valentine's Day telling you that I did not like it in hopes that you would like me. I was the one who was afraid to read in class because reading evaded me and gave me my biggest problem, lack of confidence. So when I lost my two front teeth in a hockey game and couldn't get them fixed for two years, I got to know what lack of confidence was really all about. And it followed me through most of my life. Whenever I had a chance to do something important I doubted myself. So what happens to you as a kid does follow you. I'm sure of that.

I was the little kid who dreamed about playing football for the Ohio State Buckeyes. The one who always wondered what was going to happen to him. And of course, since I was low man on the totem pole, I didn't mind making fun of anyone below me. I only talk about this as I think there were many kids just like me.

And I didn't like structure. Not to the point that it turned you into a robot. Yet, in the military rules and regulations are a way of life. I guess I can see the paradox in myself as in most people. I guess the question is was I unable to fit in or was it the system? If and when that happens, is it the kid's fault or is it the fault of the education system in place at the time? Modern educators now realize that not every child learns at the same pace and in the same way, therefore, for some it is impossible to keep up in the classroom. Does that mean they are stupid? Or backward? Not necessarily, it is just that they have a mental make-up that is a bit different than others. Today all schools have made a place for "Special Needs," kids to learn at their own pace and in their own way.

For me not being able to read and write well led pretty much to my failure at every other subject in school. Without these basic skills under control I was unable to master the other subjects leaving me feeling less than adequate.

For a long time the feeling of self-loathing that my educational shortcomings gave me was a problem, and it took a long time to overcome it.

Back to my American idealism. At the height of my idealism I still believed that things like burning draft cards and burning American flags was wrong. The very idea of it stirred me to an intense distaste of the people who practiced it. I was not really in the tank for the U. S. Government, as I abhorred the killings at Kent State. Many thought it was an act of the government rather than the accident it probably was. But whatever it was, I hated the reality of what happened.

How is it that no matter what we do for the poor they always seem to remain poor? The fact is that during the Great Depression of the 1930s the poor and minorities of this country would seem to be at their lowest economically. Since the 60s, untold billions of dollars have been spent on the "War Against Poverty." Yet after almost fifty years of the Welfare State the poor are as poor as ever. Efforts to help seem to be bound for failure. Public housing built to house the poor doesn't take long to go downhill. A project was built behind our house in Manchester and within six months it was a dump.

Whose fault is that? Is it the people? Or the system. Or maybe both?

Today all these years beyond the Great Depression there is even more crime in the inner cities. There are even more teen-age pregnancies. Abortions are as high as ever. Juvenile delinquency has never been higher. Black males compromise more than fifty percent of the population of our prisons. Drug usage among kids is higher than ever. Alcoholism is also high. These are all symptoms of the poorest members of society.

So it has to be that throwing billions of dollars at a problem doesn't necessarily solve that problem. If Mr. Everyman, like myself, can see that we are worse off after so many years of the Welfare State mentality then that philosophy is not working. Or is it just to keep them poor enough?

I have come to see that education is at the heart of any society's development and the lack of education is what leaves countries in the dust heap of history. Nothing is more dangerous than a lack of education. For the first time in many years America does not rank high amongst the civilized nations of the world in education. In the literacy department America ranks low. Even lower in Math and Science. Many Asian countries beat us in that area.

Somebody said that Democracy is a terrible form of government but it is the best in the world. Democracy, as good a system as it is, is susceptible to the worst in human nature. It can easily be perverted by the greedy and unscrupulous for their own benefit. The blessing of American freedom helps these greedy unscrupulous types pull off their misdeeds.

So it can be seen that Democracy is flawed. Much the same can be said about Capitalism. In the movie *Wall Street*, billionaire mogul Gordon Gecko, played by Michael Douglas, uttered these words at a stockholder convention. "Greed is good. Our system thrives on greed."

Sound perverse? Not really. He's right. If it weren't for greed and the lust for the mighty dollar, our system would not work. Love of the dollar drives our economy, our industry, our lust for the best (material) things in life. But it requires incentive. In that way it is good. In Communist and Socialistic systems that feature cradle to grave social programs, incentive is taken from the people and they operate in a lethargic environment with no ambition or hope for the future. It matters not if a person does a good job or bad job, the next day he will be back at the same job with no hope of ever having anything better. So when compared to that, isn't our system of Capitalism better? I guess the answer is that it is better only in that it allows Mr. Everyman to earn more and thus live better. But somewhere along the way the system has lost its humanity.

Now, while most of us don't want to be considered greedy, most of us want to make money and buy all the baubles, bangles and beads, toys and whistles that money can buy.

So in the scramble for riches, we forget our humanity. We forget about those who need us. Those who depend on us. The poor. The oppressed. The infirmed. Compassion is not something you can teach. It is either bred into people or it is innate. Then again, I'm not really sure it can be bred into people.

Yet, as an American, I have an inbred need to support the little guy and to loathe the corrupt big shot. I'm not talking about the rich men who have earned it and help society, but the truly corrupt.

I ask myself, isn't the only reason we do not have cars that run on air is because no big shot can figure out how to make money on it? A country that can produce the technology to go to the moon and to explore space cannot figure out a more economical way to run our cars, heat our homes and fuel our industry? I don't believe that. Isn't the only reason that our houses are not run on a self-sufficient energy source is because no one can figure out how to tax it?

While our country was built on the idea of a capitalistic economy, which has done well by her over the years, the greedy Wall Street and Madison Avenue types have, like many other things, perverted the concept. Now they search endlessly to sell Americans things they really don't need.

I see the government remaining in bed with big business and one of the functions of big business and Madison Avenue is to create a demand for things that we don't actually need. Ask yourself. How did we ever get along without cell phones. Now the cell phone industry is a billion dollar proposition. How about the clothes and fads that are pushed to our kids so they can be the coolest kids at school? What did we ever do before this billion dollar industry came along?

Government makes sure that it taxes us so much that we have just enough left to live and to keep depending on big business for our livelihood. This also insures that the poor will remain poor and that the middle class will just keep their heads above water. This has gone on for too long to the detriment of the real welfare of the people.

For a country that so cherishes the idea, the very utterance of the word freedom, our country has lost its status in the world for violating that very concept. Whenever there is even a hint that we do something as odious as torture, freedom suffers. Every time this happens each one of us loses a bit of his own freedom. It seems to me that we now have less freedom than in any other time in our history and that the only group strong enough to stand up for it is the middle class.

We of the middle class are so busy trying to keep ahead of the game we have no time to march in the streets and advocate on our own behalf. There is a common feeling amongst Americans that the government does not always operate in the service of the people, but rather in their own service. We should be able to demand of our government the things that are constantly promised to us.

One final word on freedom, a cherished American ideal. Whenever we violate somebody else's freedom in any way, we diminish our own.

Closely linked to this abstract idea of freedom is truth. Now truth is a slippery concept. The Latin term for it is *veritas.* It is a glowing ideal and is also the motto of a great university, Harvard. It stands imbedded for all time on the front gate of the university. Truth is supposed to, and should, prevail over lies. In fact the Bible tells us that truth will set you free. Yet everyday one sees the liars of the world, seemingly profit from their untruths while the honest suffer.

Sometimes it seems to me that lying is the best defense against a lie. Did I get that right? Do I mean that lying can sometimes be the only way to the truth? Yes, I think that's just what I mean.

Chapter Seven

In a song, somebody said, "Love is where you find it." For me it was in my Aunt Jean's home with cousins I loved. For me it was like being on vacation from my parents. My father was a tough man, but he was fair.

So when I was thirteen it was proposed that my brother and I take an RV camper trip around the country with our cousin Jackie, her husband Bob and their toddler daughter Amy. Looking back to 1972, the only thing missing from the red Volkswagen bus with a camper top, was the peace sign.

It was so exciting! I spent every moment with my eyes glued to the passing scenery. As we headed south from New Hampshire, I could not believe that I was going to all these places. I had hit the mother-lode of adventure. And I was ready.

First stop was Amish country, near Hershey, Pennsylvania, for a look at a completely different culture. These Amish people were of German heritage and lived their lives with dignity and grace much like the Americans of the 1800s. In this modern day they refused to use such things as electricity, automobiles or any other modern conveniences. I wondered why people would forgo all the conveniences of modern life. To what purpose?

They fascinated me. I watched them as they drove their black horse drawn carriages, the horses clip clopping down the road as automobile traffic carefully skirted them. I watched them on their farms where no electric or telephone lines could be seen. I amazed at their dark plain clothing, the men in black clothing, the women in flouncy dresses and bonnets. I had truly returned to yesteryear.

In some ways I saw us camping out as similar to the Amish. There were no hotels for us. Sure, we would get a hot shower or bath at an RV camp along the way, but for us we were roughing it.

After leaving Pennsylvania we headed down the coast. When we went through the Chesapeake Bay Bridge Tunnel I was amazed at coming out of the tunnel in the middle of the bay. I thought if we can build this we can build anything. The next stop was Kittyhawk, North Carolina. This stop filled my boyish imagination with the story of the Wright brothers, a couple of bicycle mechanics who invented and flew the first airplane. It certainly stirred the imagination, thrusting me back about sixty years to the day of the fateful first flight of man. As I trudged the sand dunes of Kittyhawk I saw (in my mind's eyes) the flimsy craft leave the bonds of earth and soar into the sky for the historic 30 second flight.

As we continued south I found the change in scenery interesting. The trees of the South Carolina lowlands were covered with the drooping, hanging Spanish moss which some people likened to a beard. It was soft and dark and hung down at least a foot or more. It made the trees look so exotic and so different from my native New Hampshire, the land of the evergreen. Also, in South Carolina I was able to see some of the sights I had read about in my books. I had a new interest in American history and was riveted to the sights and sounds of Charleston, where the Civil War began. I loved the ante bellum homes along the famous Battery where the Confederate cannon bombarded Fort Sumter out in the harbor. It all came alive to me, living history in front of my very eyes.

I have revisited Charlestown and sat on the bench looking out over the harbor. For the average school kid History as a subject is a matter of memorizing important dates of battles, treaties, and political events and so on.

What it should really be is a way to learn what had happened in the past, to study the errors of the past and to resolve not to repeat them.

Were the Union soldiers fighting to free the slaves and to preserve the Union? Were the Confederates fighting for states' rights and to keep a way of life (Slavery) or were they fighting because they were all young rural people and to young farm kids, War was *the* great adventure. The flags flying, the bugles blaring, the drums beating. I've concluded that all of this, in some way, contributed to this great bloodletting.

Or were they all guided by the great ideals of the forefathers and the Constitution. I'd like to believe that. As for myself the Constitution told me that I was part of something great, something unique, and something noble. I needed something greater than myself to live by. I know that God, of course is greater than myself, but I mean something here on earth, some ideal to live by. And for me it was the Constitution.

Maybe some save this kind of soul searching for their later years, but I decided to do it at age fifty.

Next came the Okefenokee Swamp of southeast Georgia and northeast Florida. Here was a truly exotic place. We camped beside the murky waters and from time to time were rewarded with the sight of alligators splashing out of the water or sunning themselves on the banks. Huge swooping cranes flew overhead. Snakes and other reptiles could be seen slithering around. We kept a healthy distance from them. It was fascinating to watch the native Georgians zipping around the swamp on their huge fan driven air boats. Whenever they went by we were sure to see disturbed wildlife emerge from the swamp. And as a kid I was waiting for the creature from the black lagoon to come out and get me.

All the while we traveled I was interacting with Jackie, Bob, Amy and my brother Richard. I carried Amy in a pack on my back as often as I could on hikes. There was no pressure for me and I liked that. It was a happy family and we were all having fun. We had sort of a routine at each stop where everybody had some chore to do regarding our campsite. I felt like a pioneer on a wagon train and took the chores with enthusiasm.

We headed southwest. By the time we passed through Mobile Alabama I was feeling like a seasoned traveler with my eyes open for new sights and experiences.

As we continued west towards New Orleans, I tried to conjure up everything I had read about this famous city at the mouth of the Mississippi delta.

New Orleans didn't let me down. It was a fascinating place full of Old World charm and a myriad of languages ranging from Cajun French to Spanish to the Southern drawl. I marveled at the breadth of the mighty Mississippi delta where it emptied into the Gulf of Mexico. There were river boats tied up and sailing the delta were replicas of the old time river steamboats. All in all it was fascinating. It's great how kids get into a campground and within one hour be at the playground talking to other kids about where they all came from and describing things that had happened where they live. I learned a lot about hurricanes, seeing that Camille had come through there a couple of years before and they wanted to know about snow. Most of the time, we had solved all the worlds' problems before 8 pm, when we had to get back to the camp site.

Texas was vast. From the pine covered hills of East Texas to the plains of the Rio Grande Valley was a never ending panorama of changing scenery. It was Texas, Texas Texas for days. We went to Houston to see the Houston Astro Dome. It had just been built, and it was huge. We also found out why cowboys wear chaps. We were riding horse back in a canyon and Jackie was wearing shorts. I have no idea what kind of plants they were but they could scratch petty good. By the time we got to Amarillo I felt like a cowboy so I acquired a cowboy hat and felt like part of the land. When I got back home my friends started to call me Tex. I had fallen in love with the west.

In Santa Fe, New Mexico with the wooden side walks, I felt I needed a 6 shooter and spurs on my boots. The American West of my imagination passed by mile after mile. I saw Indian reservations where stone faced Sioux, Arapaho and Navajo sat by the roadside, working the tourist trade. While they weren't the Indians of my imagination they were genuine. I also did my best at reading Buried My Heart at Wounded Knee and wondered how a nation that believed in life and liberty could have done such things. I enjoy reading old encyclopedias. They talk of those Indians as savages. I often wonder what history will say about us.

And the moment we were all waiting for. We drove all night to get there. The GRAND CANYON. We were parked on the rim when the sun came up. It was just like a movie. We sat there for awhile, it was more than I had ever imagined. We were supposed to go into the canyon on mules, but that did not work out, so we walked down and met some really nice people. I did not hear the adults talking, but I do know they did not want to go hiking the next day. That walk up was hard. I would have never admitted to it then, but I was fine with that. We only had two days there. To this day I want to go back and ride my bike on the rim. It was a trip Pudgy and I had dreamed about taking on our bikes.

I was awe struck by the grandeur of the Grand Tetons in northwestern Wyoming on the east edge of the Rockies. And I found Jackson Hole interesting with its arch of antlers, that I called Antler Park.

Yellowstone National Park was, for me, a Disney World of sights and sounds. I had never seen woods that had not been touched. I wondered how the animals could get through with all the trees down everywhere. The bears were not out yet, since it was early June. We did manage to see caribou, elk and buffalo roaming at will. Everywhere was the tall lodge pole pine that reminded me of a taller version of New Hampshire pine.

There are ten thousand hot springs in the Park, of which three hundred are geysers, including Old Faithful. We all sat there and watched Old Faithful spouting. It was ok, but nothing like the wildlife that was all around. It is definitely a must see, but for me, watching water come out of the ground is just ok, I guess.

In the Black Hills of South Dakota, we rode on horseback where Sundance did. I had my cowboy hat on. We were all riding along, and of course I was last. I did not like to be rushed. I wanted to enjoy every moment. When a porcupine came walking in front of me, I made some kind of funny noise that made everyone turn around and look at me. Jackie finally said "Arthur, are you ok?" It was only one of several times on the trip that I looked really stupid. Have you ever noticed that you seem to remember your most embarrassing moments with clarity?

Then we went into Rapid City, where there had just been a flood. I had never seen anything like it before. Buildings with two walls and a roof and nothing else. We went into the Badlands where we set up camp in a campground for the night. As we were making supper, we could see the clouds coming and the owner of the campground came and told us we should pack up all our stuff and wait the storm out in side the VW bus. I thought to myself, it can't be that bad. Luckily for everyone I was not in charge. And just like in a movie, we packed everything up just in time and sat inside the VW as it swayed back and forth. I was scared to death. Thank God it did not last that long. After that, I knew why they called them the Badlands.

We headed north into Canada and completed the trip by heading east across Canada through Ottawa, the capitol with its stately Parliament buildings on to Toronto on the Great Lakes and finally home to New Hampshire. I was happy to be home but within a couple of days I was ready again to embark on another adventure. What I have come to learn is life is always an adventure. It's merely one's own reality about it. Sometimes we laugh, sometimes we cry, but we have to keep the adventure going.

The journey had taken thirty days, a period which would live in my imagination and my heart forever.

Chapter Eight

Maybe life is like a game. I envision God telling me, "Art it's your turn. Go on out there. You're in the game."

I would say back, "But God, I don't want to go into the game. It's safer here on the sidelines."

But God insisted. "Go on in Art. It's your time."

I'd say, "What do you want me to do, God?"

He'd tell me, "Just do what you do, Art."

"But God, "What do I do?"

"I'll be right here beside you, guiding you. Don't be afraid. Go on. Get into the game."

So Art spent his whole life trying to do. My life has been a strange place. My first truck accident was the night before I was leaving for summer camp in 1990. I had just become a platoon SSgt, a job I had wanted for a long time. It seems to me that when I am not on the right track something happens to change it. I never got to camp and soon after I retired. My second truck accident happened as I was coming home from work. My truck flipped over and I was thrown from the vehicle, again not hurt. Why? I landed in a swamp, sitting up. I wish I had video. I felt so calm in the truck as it rolled over and over. Visions of my life did not pass before me. There was such a sense of calm, it felt as if something was right with me. When I became self aware I started to cry. I don't know why. I was just sitting in the swamp, looking at my truck on it side. For some reason my life is going on. That accident is the reason I started to write the book, but as I have mentioned, I am not very good at writing. I always wanted to write, but I needed help. I found help in the form of a ghost writer, and also my wife. She loves to correct me anyway, so it has worked out well for her too. What I am really saying is I am slow and apparently I need a kick in the ass sometimes. And the forces are more than willing to give it to me. They have been easy on me compared to others.

I have not mentioned a lot of my family. I have a lot of first and second cousins that I love very much. When we all get together we have a blast. There is one that stands out above all the rest, Pricilla. When I was small, I was so afraid of her. She is older than me and there was something quite different about her and two of her other sisters. They were mentally retarded. Now Pricilla lives on her own and the other two are institutionalized. She comes ever year to the family reunion and over the years I have gotten to know her well and find that she has a heart of gold. If she starts laughing, I can't help but laugh with her. She stays at our home or stays with Nita, one of my other cousins, in a nearby hotel. One day recently, I asked my self, are we equal? The only answer was, yes and no. Are we equal in intelligence? No. But our souls must be equal, so we must be all equal in the eyes of God. Pricilla and Nita have become good friends. Sitting at the table one evening, I told Pricilla that as a kid I was afraid of her. She laughed and said that was crazy. Anyone can lean a lot of the intangibles from Pricilla and Nita. I know I have.

I'm sure we all are born with the innate ability to distinguish between right and wrong. Pricilla has taught me that. I oftentimes wonder if I grew up in a hard place would I be writing this now? For example, I know that if I were a Mexican of the lower class and I knew that by slipping across the border illegally I could help myself and my family, I would do it in a heartbeat.

Now something about important friendships in my life. As I've mentioned Pudgy and I go way back to our high school days. Although at the time I thought it was perfectly normal, life and its rigors have taught me that having a good friend is a rare and wonderful thing. I can make an enemy in about five seconds but it takes years to develop a good and enduring friendship.

Pudgy and I bonded as we went through life together from kids to young men to not so young men. He lived next door to Doreen and they had known each other since they were eight or nine.

As for him and I, maybe opposites do attract. He was flamboyant where I was conservative. He was a gambler. I wasn't. We even picked distinctive branches of the military in which to serve. He enlisted in the Marine Corps, considered showboaters by the Army, and I, the ultra conservative, enlisted in the Army Reserve.

He was the kind of guy who would walk up to anyone and begin a conversation, something I could not do. Nor was it in my personality to do.

He was even showy on the road. He would pick up hitch hikers but his driving was so fast and reckless that they were soon begging to get out. He would put his E brake on at 50 mph and see if he could make a bat turn. Or do 90 mph down a one way street. *The wrong way.* These were, of course, high school days when all high school kids did something like this one time or another. Our bonding was such I would just say "Hey Pudgy, that was real smart. You really didn't need that car anyway". Luckily and through the grace of God we both survived those years.

We had a knack for knowing each other's moves that only people who are truly close can understand. When we played basketball I could guess where to put the pass knowing he would be there to get it and vice versa. That kind of bonding is rare.

But it wasn't until we experienced the romance of the open road on our motorcycles did we really understand the affinity between us. We used to ride so close together that we could talk. We could almost read one another's mind and I'm sure there was a mental telepathy between us so that we could guess what was happening up ahead of us and relay it one to the other. We rode so close sometimes that we could lean over and hit the other's kill switch. There was an easy going camaraderie on the road that I will always remember. We were the Butch Cassidy and Sundance Kid of the road. After all it's a short hop in the imagination from riding to biking. The feelings are much the same. These are feelings of the open road and friendship that will remain etched in my memory forever. Especially since Pudgy died.

It was in the cold dead of winter in January of 2003. He had asked me and Doreen to go with them to Foxwoods Casino in Connecticut to gamble. He loved to gamble while I was not much of a gambler and so we declined.

He died at the tables, up by four thousand dollars. I always marveled at the scenario and thought what a fitting way it was for him to go.

I still remember the nightmare ride (I call it the ride to Hell) to the Connecticut hospital to pick up his wife, Katie. Pudgy was well aware of his condition as was I. I was always warning him about it. But Pudgy moved to the beat of a different drum. He was dead when we arrived and like one soldier to another I kissed his forehead and said goodbye. It was heart wrenching.

Though he died in January he wasn't buried until May. I parked my bike next to my porch for a week. Every day of that week, a small bird perched on the bike. Of course I saw it as significant. A connection to the other side? After the funeral the bird never returned. I didn't ride much for a couple of years.

Pudgy and I watched out for each other. If one of us was drinking too much the other would stop. We would go out on our bikes for four hours and manage to go only twenty miles or so, stopping for a drink, for a smoke, to talk. Anything. It was just something we loved to do together.

We rode together so often that after he died; people told me that when they saw me ride by they were certain he would be right behind. That was our image, always together. I kept the bike I had used to ride with him for five years, although it was barely ridden the last three years. When I finally mustered up the courage to sell it there were tears in my eyes. I don't know if the tears were for days gone by, for myself or for Pudgy or who knows. Maybe it was for all of it. Thirty years of friendship that will remain etched in my heart forever.

Pudgy's wife and my wife were friends and so we would all take off in the motor home, pulling our bikes some place and riding for the weekend. The girls did not like long rides on the bikes. That was fine with us since we didn't want them with us anyway. Our riding was a macho trip. No doubt about it. We felt like the ultimate buddy movie with the bikes as our connection.

I have again taken up riding, but course it's not the same. My new bike has a radio and that what keeps me company. I do ride with my family more. A lot of us, including my sons, have bikes and I enjoy that quite a bit. When one looks back and knows that everyone behind you is of the same blood and there are 15 motorcycles and a mere 7 years before, some of us did not even know each other, it is quite an overwhelming feeling. The family reunion has brought us all together and that is pretty cool. I still ride a lot by myself and when I find myself stopping at the rest area in Epsom, I realize that I am trying to return to those carefree rides that Pudgy and I took together. It's so sad to realize that they are gone forever. But I have to admit, the memory isn't gone. Not even for the short term.

On the other hand I did experience other friendships. One that was quite different for the likes of me. I know an older woman, Roberta, for whom I did construction work occasionally. She had experienced a tornado recently. She's 78 years old and her birthday is the same as mine. She is very intelligent and has a completely different background than me.

The tornado just missed hitting her house. The only damage was a branch through the window. Nobody was hurt but it was still traumatic for her, her daughter and grandkids. I helped out with her clean up. Ordinarily I would spend at least two hours working and six hours talking to this very special lady. She gave me the strength to keep going when the bad economy destroyed our business and when we lost most of the equipment to foreclosure. She helped me keep my head up high.

When I learned of the incredibly difficult times she had faced and endured in her life it made my own problems pale by comparison.

It seems that whenever I need it God sees to it that someone special enters my life to help me over the rough spots. I often think about where I would have been without people like Butch, Jackie, Mom, my dad and others in my life who were always there with great kindness and support. And while I did not always take their advice, I was nonetheless, grateful for it. They taught me that anyone who takes an interest in you should be special to you and they should be treated as special

As for Roberta, I will take the wisdom she imparted to me, to the grave. Some people will tell you that friends come and go but someone like me will tell them that no, good friends are eternal.

This book has been heart wrenching for me, bringing back good and bad memories. A lot of the people I have talked about are gone. My father, Butch, Pudgy, all of my aunts and uncles on my father's side. All people that have given me life and hope. But there is another group that gave me the chance of a lifetime, a job. Not just any job, a job that turned into a family. They started me out as a laborer and had faith to make me a foreman and then a superintendent. If you remember, I was really hoping for something to show up and it did. I first met Mark in the Army Reserves. He knew that I was union and said that he could keep me working for 10 months a year. As you might know, that is hard to do in construction. So I took the job. It was better pay, but I had to travel at least two hours a day, sometimes more. As the years went on, Mark became more like a big brother to me. He would often yell and scream at me. He was under a lot of stress. We had the best people working there. Lenny, Bobby, Dennis, Leo, Moose, and I worked hard and they all taught me a lot. We installed water, sewer and drainage pipe and I became good at what we did. With Mark's brother Mike in the office and good crews in the field we plowed ahead. On the job my name sometimes became Art Dow. I went to some of their family functions and I thought this is how work should be, friends caring about each other and doing good work along the way. It was just like family with plenty of love-hate relationships. One day we want to beat the hell out of each other, the next day we were drinking beer and laughing. I only mention this because I learned a lot more than just construction there. Mark was not unlike me, he had something to prove. He was smart and as far as I knew, he could figure how to do most anything in construction. And so for almost twenty years, I worked there and when I left, I knew it was time to move on. I was getting tired of driving to some jobs five hours a day, sometimes more, plus eight or more hours on the job. When my oldest son got sick, I realized that I had not spent much time at home. I needed to spend more time with my family. I came home.

I miss their friendship and our long talks in the office. I think of them often, Mary, their mother, and Mike and Mark and their kids who I worked with. And I only wish them the best.

Chapter Nine

Some observances of our culture and its evolution.

We moved to Northwood in 1974. It being a small town, and coming from the largest city in the state, was a culture shock. The school looked like a gym attached to a large farm house. The kids were strikingly different than where I came from. Walking in the hallways at Memorial High was more like a rat race with kids bumping in to you, hitting your books and having them fly all over the place. One did not have to be on guard walking down the halls at Coe-Brown. At Memorial, I did share my locker with the prettiest girl in the school, Jackie. No, I never dated her, but I wanted to. That's the way life worked for me. The friendliness of the kids at the new school was refreshing to me. As I met kids and played on the basketball team, something that would not have happened at Memorial, I just wasn't that good, I grew to be very comfortable at this school. Most everything was different. There was winter carnival with arm wrestling, pie eating, snow shoe races, basketball and so on. We made maple syrup and showed cows at the fairs during school. Where I came from, we did not even go to the fair. For a kid who never even touched a cow before and with Patty making me laugh in class, I was off and running to a whole new beat. I liked these kids. Even the teachers seemed to care, a concept that I was not used to. Don't get me wrong, there were some good teachers at Memorial, it just seemed to be different with less students. Maybe fewer students are a better concept.

Out side of class was just as strange. It did not take long for the police to know my name and just about every other car on the road was someone you new. All the time thinking to myself this is pretty cool. Jerry, the chief stopped me once and said "Do you know what I do to drunk drivers?" I said "No". He dragged me out my car, threw me on the hood and held my head down and said "This is what I do to drunk drivers". I said "OK, Jerry I won't do that". He got back in his car and left. I thought to myself that this guy really likes me, he cares. In 1975 I did not think it was harassment, he was seriously joking, if you know what I mean. As time went on, if we were going to have a party, we would go to see the chief to let him know, and he would always say "I will be down to check on you and there better not be any drinking and driving." Today we make criminals out of our kids, when they are only doing what we did as kids. People can say what they want about our police chief, he knew what his job really was and that was to keep the kids safe, you can't stop them from doing what kids do. But if you know where 80% of the kids are and make some of them responsible, that's not a bad thing. The problem today is the police would go to jail for doing that. Just because some 17 year old had a beer? I'm thinking 5 to 10, what's your thought? [The drinking age was 18]. There is no such thing as personal judgment; the laws have made that clear. It was a good time and place to grow up, I must say. The only down side to a small town and school is that no matter what you did every one in the school knew about it the next day. I dated a girl after a basketball game, I think we went parking, I can't say too much my wife is going to read this. Just joking. Anyway, I guess we stayed out too late and her father, who was a cop in the next town over, came to my house looking for me in his uniform. My parents thought that something had happened to me. Well anyway, they did not know where I was. The next day everyone in the school knew every detail. All and all I think I was part of something really special. The kids that lived here their whole life probably did not see it like I did. I felt like I belonged here, at home, in school, you knew all the cops, you did not look at them as the enemy. And all the kids got along. What a concept.

So to me culture is led by leadership. It creates the tone, a way of thinking, as with teachers and police. I came from 40 miles away and the culture was not the same. Why? More people, more problems? Was the tone different or did I change? Now schools are in a sad state of affairs with police at the doors. Schools in lock down. There seems to be a problem. I don't have the answer but what I do know is if there is water bubbling out of the ground from a water main, you could dig a trench and give the water some place to go, or dig up the road and fix the problem. We do seem to like to dig trenches. That 'no kid left behind thing', we may have found them. Being a parent, I can't begin to tell you what great sadness comes over me each time I hear about the death of a student at the hand of another. There is something dreadfully wrong.

I'm sure that government policies affect our culture, but I am also equally sure that government policy doesn't affect our culture as much as trends, fashions and new gadgetry. I have mentioned the explosion in cell phones and Ipods that has hit our society. Again, what did we do for communication before this? It used to be that only somebody important with important needs had this type of communication. Now everyone seems to need one. You see it everywhere. The other day in the supermarket I observed this scene. A guy is shopping and talking to his wife. "Yeah, honey. Do you want the peeled tomatoes or the tomato paste? Do you want skim milk or whole?" This is hardly important stuff. But we have become used to it. People are constantly talking or sending text messages about the most mundane stuff imaginable.

The government, of course, gets into the act when they see a need to moderate it. Like talking on cell phones while driving. There has been an increase in car accidents while people are talking on cell phones, so now in many states it is forbidden.

But it was not government policy that fueled the need for this type of communication in the first place.

Now take driving. We live in a harried society where most families have a working wife. This means the old job, tough enough as it is, of housewife and mother needs to be combined with a full time job in industry. Consider the extra stress this puts on families and family life. Many of these working families have pre-school children who need to be dropped off and picked up at day care centers. More added stress.

Then look at the increasing tax load on the middle class. While everyone is struggling to achieve the American Dream he also has to struggle to keep up with his bills and the tax man. More stress.

How is that stress expressed? On the road for one place. On the road today there is little courtesy and even less patience. People cut one another off. Looking back I can say that at one time or another I too am guilty of this type of bad behavior. I tried to get to the root of the behavior because when I got in my car twenty minutes ago I was happy, now I am pissed off. Because I let some ignorant person ruin my day. I was infuriated with the one finger salute they gave me because they were unhappy with something I had done or had not done or had not done fast enough for their taste.

I have made a conscious effort to not let road rage ruin a perfectly good mood and an otherwise good day. As for the other drivers who continue with this behavior, they just have not analyzed their lives yet or have come to a place in their lives where they realize what a waste of energy and temperament road rage really is. Come on folks, we should all be friends, not enemies. Look at how foolish road rage is. We are so willing to die for each other, sending our kids into battle, burying them and honoring and crying for them, but we don't seem willing to let a fellow American in at a traffic jam or to help out when the house burns. We need to become part of the solution and not part of the problem.

Some thoughts about war and our government's decisions to fight certain wars. Someone said that wars are started by old men but fought by young men. We, as American citizens, need to keep reminding our government officials that they should do everything and I mean everything humanely possible before deciding to put American kids in harm's way. I understand that we have a completely voluntary military but that shouldn't be an excuse for the politicians to send them in harm's way without the utmost provocation or the belief that there simply is no other way. Ideals are necessary, no cultured people could live without them, but when every election year politician speaks of change all I can observe is *where is this change*. In my lifetime I have never seen any of it.

More thoughts on God and my relationship to Him. I think everyone can benefit by getting away sometimes from the dogma of their religion. I often times will kind of forget everything I have been taught and do my own thinking about God. I hate to see his name used frivolously to justify hate and wars. I hate to see the God of my religion belittled by the commercialization of certain holidays like Christmas and Easter.

I tend to believe a writer like Joseph Campbell who tells us that the world's religions are less disparate than we had believed and that they have more in common with each other than we had realized. With some nuances, some subtle, some not so subtle they all preach pretty much the same human values. It's in the interpretation that we have problems. It's like I said before, my religion, Christianity, teaches that "thou shalt not kill." Yet there are all kinds of exceptions. The Muslim Koran tells its readers to "kill the infidel." Infidel by the way is you and I and anybody who is not of the Muslim faith. Now is that a finite interpretation? Most agree it is not, yet for those whose purpose it fits, it is a finite interpretation, thus killing any infidel is pleasing to the Muslim.

It's the Dogs of War who preach this kind of thing for their own purposes, and I'm afraid that the only way to thwart it is by education. One can only be successful with these kinds of lies through ignorance.

For me any common man can see that the religions of the world are interpreted the wrong way is because it benefits some leader or some cause or some movement. A simple person can see that no Divinity would preach killing those, who are in effect, God's children.

For me life, and serving God, is about small kindnesses. Not necessarily the big things, as important as they are, but the more everyday things. Somebody is searching for a pen. I lend them one. Somebody is stuck on the road. I stop.

How do I or anyone else know there really is a Divinity? A God? Because of the dreams and the intuitions and the feelings one has at certain times. For me it was the eagle dropping his feather, the bear staring me in the eye, the hand that guided me to the lost boy, or a tiny bird on the handle bar of a motorcycle, and more. Sometimes they are subtle and take some analyzing, but I think the conclusion will be to realize that there is a God and no doubt He is in your life. And he is encouraging you to live His way, the way of peace and love and compassion.

I believe it is important to pray for the dead. In my religion we pray for the repose of the souls of the dead. That is when I think of my seventeen aunts and uncles who have passed on. After all it is the condition of our souls, yours and mine that we should be most interested in and our souls will only rest in peace if we have lived our lives the best way we know how.

In this effort I try to stay away from people with negative energy. One can only be brought down by them. On the other hand think about how good people can make you feel. People who are friendly and happy and full of life.

My comments about the stress of family life in the twenty first century was not just rhetoric, since I lived it myself. At one point in our lives my wife, Doreen and I decided that she should quit her job and we would live on one income. At that point I had been working long days and my home life and my social life suffered. Old friends thought we didn't want to see them anymore.

So the decision came that I would be the breadwinner. But being a breadwinner has its own pitfalls and dangers. One was at the mercy of the economy, fuel costs, personal accidents, fate and a lot more. Everyone didn't automatically succeed in everyone's version of the American Dream. Some of us lost the dream and had to fight our way back to it. I even had to consider that maybe the American Dream wasn't for me. Maybe it had too many strings attached. Maybe the price one had to pay was too high. Maybe one could be happy without it!

But we made our own little American Dream. Doreen and I had purchased a 1958 trailer in 1979 and found a place for it in a trailer park. The first few winters were tough, there was no work in construction. Having to buy special formula for Josh and diapers kept money in short supply. Meals became kind of a joke for us. Even if we ate macaroni and cheese and then cheese and macaroni the next night, that was two different meals, and we would make fun of that. In some ways, they were the fun times. We had food and heat, and the roof only leaked when it rained, and we were OK. Sometimes I really take offense when people talk about people in trailer parks. For me, even at the age of 22, no one had given me or Doreen anything and that's the way we liked it. I knew that for me to be happy I needed to make it on my own. Some people get to start out with a house, maybe their parents helped them or they had a good job. Starting at the perceived bottom, (which it wasn't, we could have been living under a bridge!), can give one a much different perspective going forward. In looking back, when I pass a place like that, I think to myself, "There are probably good people living there doing the best they can". That is more than I can say about some other people. Though who would have imagined that we could have owned our own company that grossed more than two million dollars and lost it when the economy went bad. So trailer parks are a place that people can talk about to make themselves feel better. For me it a place to start a dream. Friday nights were special for us, once a month we would rent a VCR and a couple movies and go comatose on the couch. This Friday night tradition eventually turned into a dating mode for twenty eight years. Friday nights were a place to talk about everything. We cried, we laughed and we had our best fights on Friday night. One really didn't know what was going to happen. We gained respect and understanding for each other and set ourselves free on Friday night. Trust is the hardest thing to get and hold on to in any relationship. Sometime trust lived and sometimes it died on Friday nights. All and all, some of our best moments to grow as individuals happened on that one special night every week.

Chapter Ten

It is comforting to learn about oneself. As a teenager I was driven by ego (like many) and I was very selfish (like many) and I was afraid that people would hurt me since I was so shy. This was the reason why in those days I didn't include girls among my friends. There was too much possibility of being hurt by girls. I kept them at a distance and kept my heart safe and unhurt.

I never understood girls and I could never figure out whether they liked me or not. Or if they did like me, why?

Doreen and I lost contact after I left for the Army. She still had one more year of high school and as things happen, she got pregnant. Although she thought she was doing the right thing by marrying Josh's father, in the end it was not. Pudgy and I went to the wedding. Yes, it is a small town. I saw Doreen look at me like "what the hell are you doing here?" We had not been invited. As I said, it's small town. We were fated; there is no other way to say it. We were just meant to be.

I guess we were drawn together by the things we had in common. Which is the way most friends become friends. We both loved horses and loved to ride. We were both country people at heart. I felt safe around her.

After we were married, we had a long hard legal battle when I was trying to adopt Doreen's son Josh. Josh had a variety of medical problems and his doctors advised he would not live past twenty years old. He is now thirty one. His father acted more out of pride and ego than out of love for his children, as far as I was concerned.

Josh had a condition which required him to have a tube in his stomach and for some reason his father brought Josh back with the tube out. The result was that we had to rush him to Boston's Children's Hospital to have the tube re-inserted. I had to hold him down while the doctor put the tube back in. All the while he was crying, screaming at me to save him. With tears in my eyes, I wanted to kick his fathers' ass.

At the legal adoption, his father and I finally came to a grudging understanding and we had a beer together. For males of our class, a burying of the hatchet. I recall his hands shaking as he signed the final adoption papers. He told me that he knew I would be a good father to his child. For a guy who I had wanted to kill, I could now feel his pain and what he considered the shortcomings of his marriage and of his life. Of course it was kind of a practical matter for him. His choice was that someone adopted his child or he went to jail for non support.

The pain that affects Josh's mother and I is that he is a talented guy and whenever he is on the road to something wonderful and sickness strikes, we wonder if this is the last illness for him. In that respect, we have learned to cherish our kids more. Every day he is on earth is a blessing for us.

His brother Alex is seven years younger. Josh is the person who fixes things in the family; Alex is the one who breaks them. Josh isn't a big guy, weighs barely one hundred pounds. So Alex, who is twice his size, is his protector. A kid with a good heart, his ego leads him to trouble more times than not. As with many kids, the ego is used to hide his fear until real confidence comes along. Alex is more like me when it comes to reading and writing. When one is not successful in school, one does other things to make up for it.

When I compare my role as a parent to my own parents I find personally, that wanting to give kids more than we had was not such a good idea. My own parents gave me what they could afford and what they thought I needed. The rest I would go without.

In retrospect, like all kids, I never really needed all the things I wanted. Like the skates, the need was over rated. In fact not having all the things I wanted required me to be inventive and unique in finding ways to have fun.

Maybe I gave my own kids more than I should have, maybe less. That was for their own good. But as I have learned in life, we all have to learn in our own way.

An incident of my youth came back. I was working with my father on a job. It was raining. A lot of people were therefore going home. I started to join them. My father said, "Where are you going?"

"Home," I told him. It's raining!"

"Those people," he said, motioning to those departing, "don't put food on your table. Get a raincoat and get back to work."

While I didn't appreciate the lesson at the time, I do understand it.

But this was the kind of worker he was. While he was on the job not much could deter him from finishing it. A pet peeve I have about the government is that my father had a horse fall on his leg while riding. The leg broke in 7 places. Two months later, the doctors told him it was all healed. He walked on it for a couple of days and while he was walking it broke again and the doctors found other problems. He filed for Social Security and they denied his claim. He eventually lost the leg. For a man who paid into the system his whole life, a man who was a war veteran, he had to hire a lawyer to get what was justly his. And for the privilege he had to pay a lawyer 20%. WHAT IS UP

WITH THAT?

My parents, products of the Great Depression, worked for the necessities of life. Lots of leisure stuff and toys weren't a factor to them. My father would give my brother and me a dollar each on Saturday so we would leave him alone to sleep on the couch. Little did we know that was all his spending money for the week. I know it made my mother mad.

My father had one wish in life that overrode all others. He wished that my brother and I would never face combat. I'm sure this was due in part to his own feelings about having seen the horrors of war. Seeing his friends killed, mutilated and frozen to death in the icy wastes of Korea.

In that way, at least, he did get his wish. I think my father made me into a soldier at an early age. I always asked myself why and the only answer I could come up with is that there are always battles to be fought and a soldier must be ready to meet the challenge and the sacrifice. More than any other profession or vocation in life it's a soldier's lot to have to do things he does not want to do

So, I am a soldier more for peace than for war. I am a soldier who truly appreciates the blessings of home and hearth, family and friends. Sure if I have to die I want to die with honor. But honor has many connotations. I want to find peace in myself without fear or anger and to live and let live, to see more beauty in the world than I had before. To slow down and see things and feel them. Some might say I want to slow down and smell the roses.

Chapter Eleven

Back to history. But this time in regards to how the lessons affect those of us who go on living.

It is said that "History is written by the victors." And how true that is. In fact, in some countries there are ongoing battles about what was the true history. The loser, will, of course, slant it to his benefit. For example, even today the Japanese will not write in their children's History books that Japanese troops committed horrible atrocities during the war and we don't either. Some examples are the Rape of Nankeen, where hundreds of thousands of Chinese women were raped and murdered. Or the massacre of hundreds of thousands of Chinese who were thought to have helped the American Doolittle raiders in 1942. Now, the Japanese weren't the victors here but they are now a powerful economic entity so it is difficult to get them to tell the truth about history. Equally wrong is that the winner insists that the way he wrote it is the truth. The British write in their history books that the Royal Navy sunk the German battleship, Bismark. But the truth is that she was probably scuttled by her crew. Winning nations aren't much better than individuals in a case like this where their main purpose is to cover themselves with glory, an immature and vainglorious endeavor.

But we all know that the truth lies somewhere in the middle. As for me this middle ground requires a lot of truth, honesty and searching. We need to look higher than our need to be right. Otherwise there is no history and all the bloodshed and suffering were for naught.

A great curiosity of mine was why we dropped the second atomic bomb on Nagasaki on August 9th, 1945. Weren't the Japanese already defeated? Wasn't the war in the Pacific, in effect, finished?

I talk about people who write history. I have somewhat left my kids out of this book though there are some stories in here. We ride bikes together, what father doesn't like to do that. We laugh and joke and now we get along for the most part, but I think it their job to write their own history. It's not my job to tell all the stupid things that they did. It's their job, and I hope they will find the courage to write it.

On a different note, I do have to ask myself what my kids have taught me. Josh has faced an uncertain life and has been limited, physically, in what he could do, not knowing when his illness would get him. Throughout all that Josh has found a place being needed by fixing things and for the most part has not let his illness take him down, he made a world for himself and my wish for him is to find true love. Alex has taught me patience, I needed I lot with him as he got older. My wish for him is to find peace.

Alex was a happy go lucky kid; Josh was a bit more of a handful. One night when Josh was about four, we were all eating supper. Supper for Josh was formula fed through a tube, directly to his stomach. Out of nowhere he told me he was going to cut me and my dog with a chain saw.

I admonished him not to say things like that. He was young and fragile and I was well aware of his problems, yet I had to get through to him that talk like that was not acceptable. I tried to stoop to a level that he would understand. Not that I'm any child psychologist, but that was my take on it, so I said, "Josh, if you don't stop that kind of talk I'm going to pour this glass of Kool Aid over your head."

He just looked at me. Then as if in defiance he continued. I dumped the Kool Aid over his head.

The shock effect was such that he never said anything like that to me again.

While I took a lot of heat from Doreen over this, I believe this was a water shed (pardon the pun) in our relationship. Because of his health, and the uncertainty of his lifespan, the boy was allowed a lot of leeway that no other kid would get. And like any kid he pushed things as far as he could.

My common man mind told me that if he didn't stop this kind of thing and if we didn't reel him in now, he would get worse as he got older.

It must have worked because we have developed an understanding that lasts till this day.

One incident comes to mind when Josh was in first grade. I went to see the teacher, no doubt filled with memories of my own school day problems. They wanted to put him in Special Education. We refused. Adamantly. And I was thrown out. I felt like I had been thrown out of a hockey game for a display of bad sportsmanship. Except in this case it was temper, the teacher's!

Its true Josh had special needs. Because of his condition he had never been exposed to other kids much. His mother read to him a lot. This was probably no substitute with inter action with other kids. But Josh was different. He screamed if a doctor was not in a white coat and tried to administer to him. After what he had been through, who could blame him?

At times he was so unruly that I had to sit with him in class all day. For any kid this has to be the ultimate embarrassment. It must have had an affect on him because he would shape up not wanting me to come back.

By the time Josh entered third grade we agreed to have him have an

IQ test. His scores suggested that he was capable of sixth grade work or higher.

Every teacher and official came to the same conclusion. Josh was bored with the level of schooling he was in. After that his school days were better for everyone from the teachers to him to his parents.

Alex was a different set of problems. He was more like me. He couldn't get the connection of one thing to another. I could relate.

It was decided that he would benefit by Special Education. Like so many decisions one makes in good faith this one turned out to be a bad one. It seems that all this Special Ed did was slow him down even further. He was only expected to do ten problems when he probably easily could have done twelve. He eventually started doing even less and this was allowed, so that as he got older he did not put higher expectations on himself. He never tried to do more or to do better.

I then spent a lot of time trying to push him to do more but the result was only a lot of arguments resulting in him being thrown out of the house. But of course his mother would come to his rescue

As for me all I could do was let him go and make his own mistakes. I think it's natural to a parent to try to prevent this but in the end, the kid has to do it on his own.

I found it hard to follow through on this but a smart lady told me that sometimes that's all you can do. She was right. Now we get along better and like Josh, they both have good souls. And are good people.

Chapter Twelve

Previously I quoted somebody who appreciated the value of true friendship. The fact that one true friend in a lifetime is a blessing. I believe that.

Now there is something about friendship between men that is vastly different from the friendship between women. I'm not saying this in any chauvinistic sense though it may, at times seem that way.

For example, it seems to me that women are friends so that they can confide in each other and console each other about their problems and in so doing lean on each other through problems. Most of these problems are romantic. Not that men don't do the same thing but men seem to believe that the confidence is unstated, as is the support. A modern saying is "I've got your back." That's kind of what I mean.

One more word on friendship and women. My wife Doreen has always allowed me to pursue things that I loved to do and I hope that I have treated her the same. Having a friendship with a woman that has lasted almost thirty years is to me a great achievement in a day and age where people jump in and out of relationships willy nilly always chasing that ultimate nirvana. My father always told me to marry my best friend, I believe I did.

I think Doreen and I have special insight into each other. Whenever she did something I really did not like, I would have to check with my real self to find out if I would have done the same thing and I think she did the same thing. And we have learned what is important and what is not.

She has always allowed me my "girl friends", like Tia and Bonnie, Robin, Angie and Adrian. Some say it is not possible to have platonic relationships with women but I disagree, because my relationship with them is all fun, teasing and strictly platonic. These women have a great respect for Doreen. Some time ago I had come to realize that friendship is more important than sex. We kid around and I have enjoyed their company very much. Besides what guy doesn't like to have five beautiful women sitting around with him.

Pudgy had been my friend for twenty nine years. Of course he still is. We first met in high school and played basketball together. As mentioned we seemed to have a psychic ability to know where each other was and what each other was about to do. Pass. Shoot. Dribble. This is the part I meant about complementing each other.

Friendship between men seems to be a marriage without the ceremony and the paperwork. You can yell at each other, call each other names and in the end admit that "maybe you are right."

Our friendship lasted till the end of his life in 2003, and in the most important ways it lives on. Maybe his memory is one of the things that prompted me to take this course or attempt, I should say, of self discovery.

Like a lot of friends we fought a lot. The reason was because we were together so much. Men are friends because not only do they have things in common, but mainly because they simply like each other. They complement each other. Pudgy and I were at times in our lives, polar opposites, and a complete paradox. At first I was conservative. I was shy. He fixed me up on dates. I enlisted in the Army Reserve. He enlisted in the Marines. When he got out of the Marines I convinced him to join the Army Reserve with me. And so we served together. Well, the rambunctious Pudgy, in order to get me in trouble, used to drive five ton trucks up high hills to see if they would tip over. No kidding! He was a wild and crazy guy.

I remember on my eighteenth birthday we went into the local bar and had a few. The waitress who carded us had been serving us for the past three weeks. Enraged, she threw us out and banned us for six months. A real problem. That was the only bar in town.

We were traditional friends in many ways. I was best man at his wedding. And naturally he was best man at mine. What could be more natural. We used my car for a limo. I had a wonderful time at his wedding, but still no date for me. He had been older than his bride to be and so when we went out drinking, while the rest of us went into the bar he would take my car and go off with her.

Pudgy had triple by pass heart surgery when he was only twenty five. He was warned many times that he had to live a healthier life style but Pudgy wouldn't be Pudgy if he listened to the advice.

Whenever he had an operation I sat with his wife until it was over. During his recoveries, I would go visit him in the Boston hospital after work. I'd leave the hospital about eleven and get home at 12.30 only to be up at 5 for work. I got his wife, Kate, a room in a hotel so she wouldn't have to make the drive.

During one period of hospitalization my wife assisted his wife in the birth of their youngest child. Things like this, I feel, help to bond. They are personal and heartfelt.

I don't say this because I think all this is extraordinary but rather to point out that this was ordinary.

A nostalgic person, I remember a lot. I continue to stop at the last rest stop we would make when we were out on our bike rides. I have a soft spot for my bike, which was so much a part of my friendship and my adventures riding with Pudgy. So when I sold it, I sold it to an older guy. I thought this was good for two reasons. First he wouldn't abuse the bike (you'd think I was selling him my horse) and second he was someone to whom I tried to relate my tenderness for the bike. He told me he understood and would take extra special care of the bike. I had tears in my eyes as I helped him load the bike onto his trailer. He now sends me pictures.

One enduring benefit of Pudgy's friendship is that I have become closer with his parents, his sisters Robin and Penny and his niece and nephew Angie and Josh. When Pudgy's brother, Tony died just three weeks after Pudgy it was yet another shock but we have also grown closer to Tony's widow, Adrian.

Chapter Thirteen

As a boy, catching small snakes and frogs was my specialty.
My mother was revolted by these reptiles and made me keep them outside, naturally.

I had a unique outlook on these reptiles. Actually I was afraid of them and by handling them I felt I was overcoming my own fear because I knew kids weren't supposed to be afraid of snakes. The little garter snakes bit but it didn't really hurt.

Once I was catching a three foot snake under a trailer and things went wrong. The snake got attached to my arm, bit me and wouldn't let go, so I killed it. Afterwards I felt terrible having killed a living thing. I felt that the snake was doing what was natural and that it was me who was wrong, who was bad, not the snake.

When my parents gave me a 35 mm camera when I was about 22, I began chasing wildlife for a photo.

I took my camera up north looking to photograph moose and deer. I loved being close to these creatures.

Now some unique info about these animals. More people have been killed by deer, yes deer than any other in North America. Then the moose. Seems like a big docile beast doesn't it? But in mating season nothing is more dangerous than a pumped up moose. He weighs in at a half ton at least and can move fast when he wants to.

Eventually I have photographed these animals as well as alligators, and all kinds of birds up and down the east coast.

During the eighties, I voraciously read books about wild life. Once when my father was recuperating I asked him to come with me. I had been stalking a particular bear. This big guy came out faithfully at 7:45 every night. When we spotted him it was the first time I had ever seen my father get really excited about something. He could hardly believe it when the bear emerged from the woods on time. My father had his video camera and I had my 35 mm when the bear clumped into sight, about thirty or so feet from us.

In retrospect I felt odd about trying to sell my photos. I don't know why. I guess I was worried about how people would look at them. Could I take direct face to face criticism? I decided to find out, so I sold some at craft fairs, although I don't know if it was cost effective considering the cost of renting space and the time that went into it. Most people don't realize how much time it takes to get one good still photo.

I spent so much time in Errol watching eagles that I would regularly get inquiries from the US Fish and Wildlife Service about how the eagles were doing there.

My crowning achievement was the picture of the loon, which made it to the front page of a newspaper. I was even more thrilled when the Boston Globe did a story with my picture in their Sunday edition, which of course is the most widely read.

There were other benefits to photographing wild animals. Occasionally I would put my camera down and just watch them for the sheer pleasure of it. I find nothing more relaxing than having my site on a bear or deer where I can observe them, and nothing was more peaceful or tranquil than sitting in the wilderness

It was hard to get away from family and business to go into the woods sometimes, but there was never a wasted day in the woods.

I also went to schools and retirement homes to talk about wildlife along with a slide show presentation. It was fun to watch the kids and the elders' eyes light up at some of the photos.

It's funny about animals. After you are watching them for a while you get very familiar with them and consider them your own personal friends. I see this on some TV animal programs where they are watching lions say and get so attached to them.

Once I was watching a female moose for the better part of the summer when I decided to sit out in the open and see what happened. This probably wasn't my greatest idea but I never said I was smart. I got to the field before her usual arrival time. She emerged from the woods. She saw me. I didn't move. She smelled the air and started a slow gait towards me. I was thinking, *this might not be such a good idea.* She came closer. Then closer still. When she was about three feet away she gazed at me with big droopy eyes, sniffed and walked on past me. It was a spiritual moment, a communion with nature and very moving.

Later I bought two more cameras and several lenses and I would take my wife and kids on wilderness camping trips in the canoe. Alex liked it but Josh wasn't so keen. When we got snowed on a little my wife too lost her interest. So it was to be just me and Alex and the wilderness. Alex was always funny. In the canoe one day in mid September, we here heading up river when we heard a sound. I looked at Alex and said "Hey, did you see something?" He said "Yes, it was a moose." "Which way was it going?" I asked. Alex replied "I don't know, I just saw his leg". We stopped and waited and out came a small black bear. We started laughing and I called him a jerk and told him that as soon as we got back, were going to have word and picture shows so that he could learn that a moose looks like and what a bear looks like. I never got a shot off, I was laughing so hard. I decided that the wilderness was a good place to teach kids life lessons The lesson I learned was that trying to be a commercial photographer took all the fun and relaxation out of it. So it was to remain a hobby for me.

I think that the woods did for me in the 80s and 90s what my bike did for my after that.

Chapter Fourteen

I think everyone has wondered, *what if I had taken a left instead of a right. Would I be the same person if I had married Val or Fran or Patty, never knowing who I really was or who I wanted to be?* Would I still like history or like to ride a motorcycle, enjoy just sitting in the woods? I once heard someone say "I wouldn't change my life at all". I have no regrets. Because I wouldn't be the same person if I changed things.

Lincoln said, "Friendship is cruel. Without it you have no love, with it great pain."

Now I know I can't change the past but what I do know is that I can change how I look at the past. How I look at my mother for example. I know that whatever she thought of herself or where she belonged in life, she had to know that she was a loving wife and mother and that she did the best she could. And no one can ask for more than that.

Have you ever sat on a rock and thought that it was a perfect seat? Why is it that some people meet and are instant friends and others feel nothing but negativity? It was kind of like the lady I saw in the dream. It was her face that day and I immediately knew who she was. Why then didn't we get married? She was the right person at the wrong time.

Timing is everything in life. Remember I met her just when Pudgy died. My godfather died the week after and I was in a meeting with her when Pudgy's brother, Tony died. She helped me through all that. She gave me the feeling that sometimes people come into your life stay a short while to help you through something, teach you something and then they are gone. I'm sure we will all meet again one day. I need to honor all the people who have been a part of my life.

I think back on all the things, all the unexplainable things that have happened to me in my life. All the accidents, the eagle, the lost boy in the woods, the bear etc.

I can only conclude that I have more work to do and that maybe I wasn't on the right track. It goes back to that *tabula rasa,* that blank slate that life is waiting to fill up for me.

Chapter Fifteen

Like most every man I guess I get to wondering if I have done anything worthwhile in life. Of course at fifty I have hardly lived my whole life and some would say there is a long way to go.

My thinking leads me to believe that I never did anything great, like old Abe, something that affected the whole world. Or the country. I've never fought in a Great War. So what have I done for God and country. Of course I have served my country but I am talking about something "great."

I know I've made my share of mistakes. More than I mentioned here so throwing stones is not a good idea. What I think is a good idea is to look back and say "that was stupid. Let's not do that again." I like to think that God might see me as down here doing my best to care for my family. Being good to my friends.

But a place in an old movie got me to thinking deeper about my feelings of mediocrity. The movie was the Magnificent Seven and it was about 7 gunmen, taken from the Japanese story about 7 similar Samurai where the warriors are hired to protect a Mexican village from forty Mexican bandits. Now, the children of the village were awed by the swaggering gun toting "Magnificent Seven." They saw them as brave and daring and gallant while they saw their own fathers, peasant farmers who had to hire them as weak, colorless, cowards. When they expressed this to one of the seven he slapped them on their butts, sat them down and said, "Your fathers are not cowards. They get up every day and toil like dogs under the sun to feed and clothe you. I could never do that. It is they who are heroes, not me. I just practice my profession but I will never be the man that any one of them is." That's paraphrasing but that's the idea. *It takes a real hero just to face the rigors of life and the challenges of being responsible for and raising a family.*

I'd like to discuss some of my let's say "queries about life." For example if a person makes a mistake and admits to it, people say that it takes a big man to admit a mistake. But when a politician makes a mistake he or she gets beat up for it, oftentimes losing their career. So as a result I have never heard of any politician actually "making a mistake." Or the Washington mentality, some call it the Beltway mentality. "If you don't vote for my proposal you are finished here." So in order to get anything done the politician has to "go along to get along." If he doesn't do something against his nature he can't accomplish things he knows are right and good. This is the story of Washington and our democracy. One needs to do objectionable things in order to achieve something good.

I was exposed to these principles of leadership in my tenure as a Union executive. The best intentions, those benefiting the members most, are sometimes compromised because of what I'll call "Fat Cat" politics. I often wondered why our Union leadership, which wanted most to have followers and members, would seem to deliberately make enemies of them. How do non union workers become scabs? And the unions become elitists.

Take the inflow of immigrants who came into my Union office seeking jobs. Some spoke bad English, some none at all. I would always tell them the only difference between you and me was my family came here on a wooden boat and you came here on an airplane. I knew they were scared, I could feel it. They treated me like I was some big shot.

I did not like that feeling. So I would make jokes to make them feel more comfortable. I felt for these people and got to know some very well. Some union members were angry that they were coming into the union, afraid that they were going to take away their jobs, when, in reality, they could only make the union stronger. And this was a union that was started by immigrants over a hundred years ago.

As a business manager I worked with these immigrants for more than two years. I also worked with the Granite State Organizing Project, a community action group that brought churches, unions and other specific groups together to talk and act on issues in the area. I enjoyed the Granite State project and I met some excellent people. The idea was to show that there were people out there who had empathy like me. I knew that if we wanted to get as many people working as we could, there was going to have to be community support. As it turned out, my own local was not ready to be a part of this kind of grassroots movement.

The president of our local, Joey, was a person, who if I didn't find, would have found me. I'm sorry to say that I left in the middle of my term and by so doing let him down. I'm sorry, because he was a good friend. I left in frustration feeling I could do no more and I could not change the things I wanted to change. I'm happy to say that we have reconnected and remain good friends; he has a heart of gold.

Union execs are, in effect, politicians and care most about their power base to the detriment of their membership.

I was getting death threats and so it was not possible to accomplish anything. I felt like I was up against an organization that I read about as a kid.

Their anti progressive thinking will not last this century. What I want to make clear is that these dire threats were coming from union members and not my superiors, nor did it reflect their views.

Let me say that I have always been a union man. My father, uncles and many cousins were all union members. The idea is that everyone wants benefits but no one wants to pay benefits to others. It costs too much.

Is that why foreign goods are so cheap? We would rather have some foreign eight year old make it? We wouldn't put up with that here. But we tolerate it with a blind eye because it is foreigner's kid. Not ours.

It brought me back to the Honduran kid shining my boots when I knew he should be in school or playing. I certainly wouldn't allow that back home. But of course this was all part of my world view education.

Part of that world view is to accept other views, other cultures and other lifestyles. What they were doing was not wrong. It was just not right for me. An American.

So I guess I am still filling that tabula rasa. I still have a lot to do and God willing, I will do it.

You know some of my pet peeves already. I hate to have family people work on Christmas and holidays. I hate seeing stores open on Sunday. Let people stay home and have time together. Families breaking down. Why? United States policy should evolve more directly from the American people. I know we have to have leaders to speak for us but if the policy is wrong, that leader should correct it. This question is deeper than I can go into here but the bottom line is the government should be more in tune with the wishes of the people.

So why is this? Because Big Business is calling the shots. And the government shouldn't be in bed with Big Business. They are because of the financial support. Again too deep a question to go into here. I watch the news about how they have to free the money up so that we can buy cars and houses, and I think that people are more worried about buying tires for the cars they already have and heating oil for their houses they may lose to foreclosure. No one is buying anything big right now. Hello! Put money into roads, dam's and bridges to get people working. Money is not like water, it only flows uphill. And the war on drugs only seems to make drug dealers rich.

While this might sound like griping I am constantly aware of the fact that only in a country like America can I gripe up these things freely. I and others have served and fought for that right. So I guess at this point in life the John Wayne of my childhood days is still with me. I don't mind. It's all going on the *tabula rasa*.

I'd like to end with a quote from Sarah Meredith. "Believing in yourself is *an endless destination. Believing you have failed is the end of your journey.*"

CPSIA information can be obtained at www.ICGtesting.com
Printed in the USA
BVOW071120160812

297967BV00002B/96/P

9 781438 938042